Kate knew the man standing before her. . . .

Kate bent down with her hand out, waiting for Mooch to bring her the stick. But Mooch didn't come to her. Instead he veered out of her sight and into the trees.

"Hey." Kate stood up and whistled. "Mooch, come here, boy."

Suddenly the stick flew out of the trees toward the beach. Seconds later Mooch bounded after it.

"Who's there?" Kate called. "Who is that?"

Kate saw someone move out of the trees.

"Hey—" Kate started to call again, but the word died in her throat. "Who are you?" The question came out as a whisper, because Kate didn't need to ask. She knew the man standing before her. Only, she had never expected to see him again.

Kate's mouth moved again, though this time no sound came out. Her lips struggled with a word, and Kate felt strong familiar arms around her, as the name caught in her throat: "Justin."

HEAT WAVE

Katherine Applegate

HarperPaperbacks

A Division of HarperCollins*Publishers*

This is a work of fiction. The characters, incidents, and dialogues are products of the author's imagination and are not to be construed as real. Any resemblance to actual events or persons, living or dead, is entirely coincidental.

HarperPaperbacks *A Division of* HarperCollins*Publishers*
10 East 53rd Street, New York, N.Y. 10022

Produced by Daniel Weiss Associates, Inc., 33 West 17th Street, New York, New York 10011.

First printing: August 1994

Printed in the United States of America

HarperPaperbacks and colophon are trademarks of HarperCollins*Publishers*

10 9 8 7 6 5 4 3 2 1

Many thanks to K.J. Adams for her work in preparing this manuscript.

ONE

"Marta, Marta, wait for me!"

Marta Salgado hurried toward the doors of Edgar Lee Middle School. When she heard her name, she turned and stopped. She stood with her hip cocked, waiting for her friend Christina to speed up her progress.

"Wait, Marta, I'm coming." Christina raced across the school yard, her smile wide, the sun flashing off of her new braces.

"You are the latest, least dependable girl in the sixth grade," Marta said, laughing. "And now definitely the shiniest."

Christina opened her mouth to show Marta the rubber bands pulling her teeth together. "Well," Christina said, "I actually think braces are pretty cool looking, but they sure do hurt."

"Yeah," Marta agreed. "But when they're

1

gone"—she jumped back and hid her eyes behind one arm—"*poof*, you'll be the prettiest girl in junior high."

Their laughter was interrupted by the loud bell ringing inside the school building. Marta and Christina looked around and suddenly realized that the school yard was practically empty. "Oops," Christina said. "First I'll be the girl with the most detentions! We'd better get going."

They ran up the front steps and heard the bell ringing again. But just as they neared the front door, they heard another sound that stopped them both short: the screech of squealing tires right behind them. Then they heard shouts, and louder sounds—popping firecrackers—and screaming.

Marta turned and looked toward Christina. She saw a flash of braces, Christina's opened mouth—her eyes full of shock and fear—and Christina falling. For a moment Marta froze, watching a pack of bodies running past, listening to the sound of their sneakers slapping the pavement. And then her eyes went back to Christina, down to where she lay on the steps. There was blood on her sweater, on her hands. Her books lay scattered at her feet.

Marta started to bend, thought she heard herself screaming something, screaming for help. Her own books dropped as she reached for Christina, but then there was more noise, more firecracker explosions, and Marta felt a blow to her back. Something slammed into her. She lost her breath, and felt as if she were being pushed forward into a crowd. But there was no one in front of her, no one to catch her, and she fell.

Marta tried to crawl her way to the school doors, but her body was numb. She couldn't feel anything below her waist. Her head was spinning, and there was Christina swaying crazily in front of her, slumped against the brick wall.

As Marta reached out for her friend, she whispered her name. But Christina's eyes were closed, her face white. For a moment Marta felt nothing. Then a breeze passed over her. She heard the rustle of leaves on the sidewalk and from far away another bell, muffled shouting and screaming, and then the pounding of running feet. And Marta's eyes closed just like her friend's.

Marta jerked awake, breathing hard and gripping the cool metal of her wheelchair to steady herself. She blinked at the first licks of bright early light—the sun rising out of the ocean. As Marta tried to gain her bearings, the terrible memory of that long-ago afternoon lingered.

It was so early, still half-dark on the boardwalk, and maybe still black over the bay behind her. Not too many people were up in Ocean City.

Not after a full day on the beach and a night of carnival rides and parties.

Marta watched the soft pink and orange stretch over the horizon. It looked as if the sky was bleeding, and she shivered, trying to shake off the bad memories. It was a little cold, and Marta's clothes were damp with dew. She'd been out all night, unable to sleep. Afraid to sleep. She'd spent the last six hours rolling aimlessly along the boardwalk.

Marta ran her hands over her face. She pushed her fingers through her long curly dark hair and twisted the mass into a loose knot at the nape of her neck. Then she looked down at herself.

She had come a long way from being that little girl in sixth grade. She knew she looked different, that most of her had continued to change and age normally. Her face had grown longer and thinner, her eyes were darker, the figure she had longed for when she was eleven had arrived. Or at least half of it had. She was well-developed on top, and strong. Voluptuous would have been the word for it, only voluptuous didn't seem a word you could *ever* use for a woman in a wheelchair.

Finally, the image of his face came into Marta's mind. The real reason she had been unable to sleep. For fear of seeing *him* in her dreams. Dominic. Dominic Velasquez, with eyes

4

that seemed to be made of the night—the endless black between stars.

It was almost impossible to believe that she had met him less than two weeks ago. Dominic made her feel like no guy ever had. No more Luis Salgado's tough daughter with a sharp word for anyone who thought she couldn't make her own way. She had let down her guard, intrigued and desperate to know what was haunting Dominic so. To know what he needed and wanted. *Maybe I'll regret this,* she remembered thinking just last night.

Last night. That was it. Last night had never ended for Marta. She had been replaying it over and over through the long dark hours of the morning.

They'd been out at the end of the pier. Dominic had kissed her, holding her so closely that all of his hunger and fear had run through them both. Marta felt as though she were flying, she felt so alive in his arms.

Then he had pulled away and left her churning with emotions. She had been furious. Where did he keep running away to? Every time they got close to each other, she could see his dark eyes hooding over.

So he wants to run, Marta had thought. *I'll make him run for me then,* and she had taken off down the boardwalk in her wheelchair, releasing all her pent-up frustration and energy.

But it hadn't helped. What she found out at the other end of the boardwalk was unbelievable—something she never could have imagined. Marta demanded to know why he was pulling back from her. Asking him if he was sorry he had fallen in love with a cripple.

But it had turned out to be more than that. On Dominic's chest was a tattoo. A symbol that had haunted her dreams: a blue snake head with a grinning skull between its fangs. The sign of the gang that had been responsible for the shooting at her school so long ago.

And suddenly there was the answer to all his reluctance.

Not only had Dominic heard of the shooting, but he had been a witness to it. And not only had he been a witness, but he had been holding one of the guns. And the gun that he'd held had fired the bullet that crippled Marta for the rest of her life.

Kate Quinn rolled away from the sun coming through her window. With her eyes still closed, she placed her hand on the chest of the man sharing her bed.

"Justi—" The word died on her lips. Kate opened her eyes, remembering who was with her and, more important, who wasn't. Her face burned and her eyes filled with tears. No, this wasn't Justin next to her. Justin—the man who'd been her first love, and her first lover.

Kate and Justin had broken up at the end of last summer, when Kate went off to college and Justin left to sail around the world, promising to return to her. But Justin could never be back in her life. Not since he had been swept off the deck of his sailboat in a storm.

It was still hard for Kate to think about him. She missed him, and she still couldn't make sense of the uselessness of his death. Justin had worked so hard for his freedom. It had always been the most important thing to him, more important than herself, Kate remembered sadly. And all of those dreams of his—of spending a free and, most of all, a full life living as he pleased and exploring the world around him—were lost with him. He had struggled so long for what turned out to be so little.

The body next to Kate shifted and muffled a contented moan into the pillow. Now, with her eyes open, Kate reached out again and knew who she was sharing her bed with. This was Tosh McCall. Tosh, who seemed her perfect other half. Tosh, who had been there with her at college. Tosh, who believed in what she believed in, who wanted to do with his life the same kinds of things that Kate wanted to do with hers, who had the same kind of ambitions and desires and goals.

This was Tosh McCall—the man Kate had finally made love to. The only other person besides Justin she had shared so much of herself with. And now the only person alive whom Kate had gotten so close to.

She thought about last night's passion. They had David's beach bungalow all to themselves for most of the night. And what a romantic night it had been—slow dancing out on David's deck, listening to the sounds of crashing waves, a canopy of stars above them. It had still been dark when they left David's early this morning and come back to fall soundly asleep in Kate's bed.

Tosh was so gentle, so special. He really had been a good friend to Kate. He had been so patient with her feelings, letting her remain faithful to Justin even though at that point all Kate had gotten from him were a few hurried letters. And then, when Kate had learned of Justin's death, Tosh had been there to comfort her, never taking advantage of her sorrow, never pushing her too far.

And last night Tosh didn't have to push at all. Kate had made up her mind. She could never expect her feelings to be completely clear-cut. Her feelings about Justin, and about Tosh, seemed destined to be complicated. Kate knew it just meant she had to take everything one step at a time.

And last night, Kate told herself, had been the next step. She lifted herself up on one elbow and ran her hand through Tosh's hair, watching him in his half-sleep. He let out low sounds of appreciation, soft moans from the back of his throat, and he reached over and found Kate's hand.

For a moment Kate was overcome by a strong sadness that a part of her life was now over. But she looked down again at Tosh, nestled into the blankets beside her, and she smiled. After Justin's memorial service on the beach, Kate had finally felt ready to go on with her life. And last night she had been prepared. She smiled to herself now, remembering where she had hidden the condom she had taken with her—taped to her own skin beneath the waistband of her skirt.

Kate had thought of Justin even then, knowing he would have laughed at her hiding place. She hoped that he could smile now, wherever he was, to see her happy and to know that she was finally moving on.

Marta watched the waves, hoping they would give her an answer. She wished she could take all of her emotions, all of her confusion, and throw it into the sea. To drown the anger before it could drown her.

Once upon a time, Dominic had done something terrible, so terrible that countless people had organized and protested, trying to find "the villain who had so ruthlessly crippled a young and innocent girl."

Marta remembered how she had begun to hate all the strangers who thought they knew who she was, knew how she felt and what she had lost. And most of all, she had hated all those who had pitied her.

"What a waste," they'd said. "She was so beautiful," they'd said. As if she no longer existed. As if she couldn't possibly be beautiful any longer, certainly not paralyzed and in a wheelchair for the rest of her life.

How little they had known her, Marta thought. How little anyone had ever cared to find out how she was *now*. Except for Dominic. He had cared. He had followed her to Ocean City to see how she had turned out.

Those same people who had made a scared young girl into a tragic heroine were the ones who had called the shooter "a ruthless, misguided villain," "an unfeeling death-machine," "a killer." Perhaps all along Dominic had been something else. Perhaps he had been a scared and confused kid, desperate to fit in, angry and alone.

And now Dominic had changed his life. He'd

straightened out, gone back to school, learned to be responsible. And he'd come to her and confessed what had happened that fateful morning.

It was the past, wasn't it? Marta thought. Maybe she should just take his answers and move on. Dominic had explained something she had wondered about practically every day of her life for seven years. An answer was a lot to get from one person, wasn't it? Marta watched the waves break softly onto the sandy beach. *Perhaps an answer is enough,* she thought. *Perhaps I don't need any more from him.*

Marta shook her head and gripped the armrests of her wheelchair. Slowly she rolled herself to the edge of the boardwalk. There was that feeling creeping up on her, the feeling of being trapped, in her chair, in this life. She shook her head again, to clear it, and pushed those dangerous emotions back.

The accident was in the past and it would stay there. No matter how much Dominic had hurt her, Marta still wanted him. And now that she knew the reason for his hesitation, knew the secret he had been hiding from her, everything was in the open. He had no excuses anymore, no cause to pull away.

"The past can't come back to beat me," Marta whispered to herself.

Marta watched the sunrise for a moment.

Some long night you've had, she said to herself. Now all she wanted to do was go home and sleep.

"Uh-oh," she suddenly said aloud. She couldn't go to sleep; she had to work the morning shift at the clinic. The summer schedule still hadn't been settled yet, and Marta had offered to take any shift open until the clinic was up to full staff. She probably had time only to go home and bathe. If she was lucky.

As she started to turn her wheelchair around, Marta saw a figure far down the beach. The sun still hadn't risen completely, and in the morning haze the figure was nothing but a dark outline. Marta could see that it was a man, the tall silhouette, the long strides, the hunched shoulders. The man was carrying something over his shoulder. It looked like an old knapsack, but even at this distance Marta could see that the bag was torn, the shadow of a broken strap waving and tangling around the man's legs.

Marta paused for a moment to watch his progress. There was something strangely familiar in his walk, familiar in his solitary outline against the sun and the water. She felt a chill run down her back and die at her waist. But the stranger was still far from where her chair perched on the boardwalk. In another moment he had disappeared completely.

TWO

Kate kissed Tosh on the cheek and slipped quietly out of bed. She went down the carpeted stairs to the main floor and crossed the foyer to the kitchen. Chelsea Lennox stood in front of the sink, spooning coffee into a filter.

"You're up early," Kate said. "That's a surprise." Kate looked at her friend closely. "So, how did your date with Steve go?"

"Oh, right." Chelsea laughed and offered a weak smile. "You mean Mr. Sensitive? Isn't that what you called him? Well, dear Kate, I think he was just a little *too* sensitive for me."

Kate wasn't sure if that was a blush on her friend's dark skin, but it sure looked like one. "What do you mean, too sensitive? Don't tell me a handsome guy like that was afraid to kiss you good night?"

"No, he certainly wasn't afraid. In fact, he offered to roll in the bushes with me." Chelsea sighed. She was wearing a bright blue sleeveless shirt, buttoned and knotted at her waist, and patterned shorts. She grabbed at the loose ends of her shirt. "Let's just say it was a case of mistaken identity."

"Who did he think you were?"

"Well," Chelsea said, laughing, "he thought I was a lot more perceptive than I am. And of course, he thought I was happily married." Chelsea sighed and frowned.

Chelsea *was* married, and sometimes it was still hard for Kate to believe it. Chelsea had been married to Connor Riordan for almost a year now. She had met him, as Kate had, when he ended up as one of their roommates last summer in Ocean City.

When they'd decided to get married last summer, Kate had been worried. There were so many reasons why it wasn't a good idea. First of all, they were both so young; Chelsea was only eighteen and Connor not much older than that. Then there was the racial issue. As much as Kate hated to admit it, it was a big deal. Chelsea was black and Connor was white, and Kate wondered if they were ready to handle the difficulties. And finally, Kate had known that a large part of their decision to get married had been so that Connor could stay in America legally.

But in the end Kate had believed that it was for love. Just as Chelsea had. And now Kate hated the nagging feeling that she had known it wouldn't work. She would have given anything not to have turned out right all along.

"So, he knew that you were married?" Kate finally asked.

"Yep, he sure did. In fact, that's why he asked me out in the first place!" Chelsea found herself laughing at the irony of it. "Can you believe it? His father is a congressman, they've got this unbelievably beige condo, and his mother definitely knows how to dress—very African-American but completely Washingtonian at the same time."

"Wow," Kate said, whistling softly. "I'm afraid to say it sounds familiar."

"You're afraid to say it?" Chelsea squeaked. "What about me? I felt like I was at home. What's so funny is that he is exactly the kind of guy my parents really wanted me to end up with. And I found out that I'm exactly the kind of girl Steve's parents would like him to end up with. What a disaster."

"I'm not getting something here," Kate said. "Why was it a disaster? If Steve is a great guy, and your parents would love each other, what's the problem?"

"Steve wanted his parents to like me," Chelsea said. She poured herself a cup of coffee and took a sip. "And he wanted his parents to think he was interested in me. But the last thing he wanted is a relationship with me. He's gay!"

Kate's eyes popped. "If he's gay, why did he ask you out?"

"This is the greatest," Chelsea yelped. "He asked me out because he thought I knew, and he thought I was safe! You know, a safe date! He's not out of the closet yet, and obviously his parents are beginning to suspect. It was the perfect opportunity to prove to everyone that he's straight." Chelsea shook her head and rolled her eyes.

"Boy." Kate winced, chuckling. "And I thought I had things to hide from my parents."

"What a joke." Chelsea laughed, and leaned against the counter. She watched as Kate fixed herself a mug of tea. Suddenly Chelsea squinted at her, taking in the rumpled hair, the sexy nightshirt, and the little smile around Kate's mouth. Her eyebrows shot up and her eyes opened wide. "I guess it's my turn to ask how your night went," Chelsea said slowly, "although now that I've taken a closer look at you, I may not need to ask anything."

Chelsea watched her friend smile, then blush, then look away.

"Well, the truth is, my night was a little bit better than yours," Kate said.

"Only a little bit better, huh?" Chelsea prodded.

"Actually, a lot better," Kate said. "It was perfect." She tilted her head thoughtfully, her blue eyes dark with memories. "It was right. It felt right to me. I think what Tosh and I have together is very special, and last night confirmed it." She laughed. "And it was certainly about time!"

Chelsea laughed quickly. Too quickly, she knew, but she just couldn't be completely happy. It was too hard to forget about Justin. And it was too strange to have him gone like that. So completely and utterly gone.

Chelsea wondered how Kate felt deep down. It's not as though she had ever fought with him, Chelsea thought. They did break up, but it had always seemed out of necessity, and from the few letters Justin had sent, Chelsea knew he hadn't forgotten Kate. From the look on Kate's face when she read them, Chelsea knew Kate hadn't forgotten Justin, either.

Chelsea sighed, and suddenly her eyes filled with tears. It was so hard to think about last summer, when they had all been so happy. Kate and Justin, Grace and David. And Chelsea herself. Chelsea and Connor.

Chelsea felt Kate's arm around her.

"Oh, Chelsea, I'm so sorry," Kate said in her ear, holding her tightly.

Chelsea let the sobs come out of her. "You were right all along, Kate," she choked out through her tears.

"No I wasn't," Kate argued. "Please don't say that."

"Don't feel bad because you were right," Chelsea said. "I'm not mad at you. I just wish I had listened a little closer." Chelsea pulled back to wipe away her tears. "But it's just that I really thought—"

"I know you did," Kate said. "We all did. But I also know that Connor really loves you. And I know that you love him." Kate grabbed Chelsea by the shoulders. "You may be having some troubles now, but don't worry. I'm sure they'll all work out."

"Thanks," Chelsea said. "I wish I could believe you, but you didn't see how he was walking with that woman on the boardwalk. I don't think Connor has the kind of luck I do. That woman definitely wasn't gay."

Kate handed Chelsea a paper towel to blow her nose. "You know that's not fair, Chelsea," she said. "You know Colleen is an illegal from Ireland, just like Connor was. And he was trying to protect her." Kate looked Chelsea in the eye.

"You're going to try and say something serious now," Chelsea said quickly. "I've seen that look before—Kate Quinn: instructor."

"That's right," Kate said. "I am going to say something serious and you'd better listen. Things are bad enough," Kate said slowly. "Don't make them worse by imagining things. Even if it's easier for you to be mad at Connor, you can't accuse him of things you know he's not doing."

"I know," Chelsea admitted, and closed her eyes. "But there are a lot of women on the boardwalk who aren't from Ireland. And those are the ones I'm worried about."

Just then they heard a whirring sound, and both girls jumped. It was the automatic elevator that Grace had had installed for Marta. Kate and Chelsea hadn't heard her come in, but obviously Marta was home, and considering the time, she was clearly heading downstairs to her room to get some sleep.

"She had a great night, I bet." Chelsea sighed. "Everyone but me."

"Chels—yipes!" Kate was interrupted and both girls jumped again as Grace's fifteen-year-old brother Bo flew into the kitchen on his skateboard.

"Hey," Kate said angrily, "you know you're not supposed to ride that thing in here. That's why you're living in the garage."

Bo rolled his eyes, and with his foot he popped his skateboard into his hands. "Now I know where Gracie's getting her new Little Miss Responsible attitude. Not that I didn't suspect it.

19

That must be why she asked you to live here this summer," he said, eyeing Kate. "So she can take lessons from you on how to be a butt-head."

"So, Bo," Chelsea sang. "So, so, Bo-Bo. What are you doing up this early?"

"Yeah," Kate added, "I didn't think the Caywoods did morning."

"Yeah?" Bo was still pushing through boxes in the cupboards. "Well, I didn't think witches were real either, until I met you."

"Score one for the Bo-man," Chelsea said. "What are you looking for, young Bo, this early in the morning? Can we perhaps help you to find anything here?"

Bo stopped rummaging and smiled. "Actually," he said, "I was sort of wondering if we had any, you know, muffins or something?"

Chelsea laughed. "I can say yes to something. But if it's strictly muffins, I'm afraid we're out." Chelsea and Kate exchanged glances.

"You have a craving?" Kate asked.

"Not exactly," Bo said. "They're not for me, really. I was just thinking that it would be nice to have muffins, you know, if someone wanted them, 'cause some people like them in the morning."

"Muffins," Kate and Chelsea said together.

"Yeah," Bo said, turning a little red.

"I'm not a big muffin eater," Kate mused, turning to Chelsea. "Are you?"

"No," Chelsea said thoughtfully, her finger on her chin. "I'm not a real muffin fan myself."

"Well," Bo said quickly, "I didn't mean you two. There *are* other people in the world." He paused. "Like Roan, for instance. If we don't have any here, I think I'll go get some. You know, for the house and all."

Bo hopped onto his skateboard and whizzed by Kate and Chelsea, heading for the front door.

"Isn't that cute," Kate said. "Bo's got a crush on Roan. It's pretty sweet to see young love like that."

Roan was a runaway Grace had found on the beach and brought home. A new project for Grace's new, more responsible, alcohol-free lifestyle.

"It's not sweet—it's unfair. Even Bo's love life is better than mine," Chelsea said.

"I wonder what they do together." Kate laughed. "I bet they look adorable holding hands."

"I wouldn't call it adorable. When I came in last night they were sitting together on the couch," Chelsea blurted out, "and they were doing more than just holding hands!"

THREE

The phone rang for the third time.

"Somebody ought to answer the phone," Roan said. She was sitting on the deck, picking at a blueberry muffin Bo had brought her. *What a great kid,* she thought, smiling. *Always nice to have a cute guy wrapped around your finger.* She'd been pretty sure last night when she'd mentioned to him she liked muffins for breakfast that there would be some for her this morning. And of course, she was right. She was an expert on human nature. Any runaway interested in a good life had to be, and Roan was definitely interested in a good life.

"Hey," Roan yelled again. "This phone is ringing! Somebody better pick it up!"

Finally Roan got up and wandered into the kitchen. She saw Chelsea on her way out the door.

"Hey, Chelsea. The phone's ringing."

Chelsea stopped short, and five or six colored pencils slid onto the floor. "Oh, shi—sugar," Chelsea said, reaching down and grabbing them. She shoved the pencils into her pocket, wrestled with her sketch pads, unhooked her purse from the doorknob, and called out, "Sorry, honey, gotta run. Can't do the phone. Late for work." She pulled the door shut behind her with her foot.

Roan cocked her head and listened to the phone ring again. Then the sound of Marta's elevator drowned it out.

Marta was coming off the platform as Roan said, "Marta, hey, listen. The phone is ringing. Don't you think you should get it?" Marta turned, her eyes flashing at Roan. "Listen, I didn't get any sleep last night, and I *work* for a living." Marta rolled herself to the front door, snatching the keys to her specially equipped van from their wall hook. "No one told me you were now queen of the nest. I thought that was Grace's position."

She rolled herself out the door. "In case you haven't noticed," she called back, "just because Grace wants to take care of you doesn't mean I'm suddenly the live-in help. Answer it yourself!" The door slammed shut behind her.

"Bitch!" Roan said to the door. "God, I

thought you were nice, but obviously I was wrong. I guess you think I should feel sorry for you 'cause you're a crip!" But no one was there to hear Roan yell, so she turned and went to the phone. "Someone must be pretty desperate to talk."

Roan lifted the receiver and propped it up against her ear.

"Yeah?" she said.

"Kate Quinn, please," a deep male voice said.

Roan heard someone coming down the stairs. "Hold on a sec," she said, and let the phone drop onto the kitchen counter.

"Hey, Kate, phone's for you," Roan said as she watched Kate hurry down the stairs in her red lifeguard's swimsuit and white shorts.

"Sorry," Kate said breathlessly. "I'm really late. Luis is going to kill me." Kate grimaced as she headed for the door. "Can you take a message? Great! Thanks a lot, Roan. See ya."

"Sorry," Roan said into the phone. "You just missed her."

"Is this Grace Caywood's house?" the voice asked.

"Yeah, sure it is. Hey, what's your name, so I can tell them who called."

"I don't think that's such a great idea," the deep voice said. "I have a feeling they wouldn't believe you. I'll try again some other time." And then there was a click, and all Roan heard was the dial tone.

"Weirdo," she whispered.

"That's not what I would call him," Grace said from the doorway. "That's much too nice a word for anyone who wakes me up. What took you so long to answer the phone anyway?" Grace moved over to the refrigerator, her matching peach-colored nightgown and wrap flowing softly behind her.

"Don't ask me," Roan snapped. "I told everyone about it, as if they couldn't hear for themselves, but they were all rushing out."

"Did I hear you right?" Grace turned and gave Roan a curious stare. "You told everyone the phone was ringing and you didn't just answer it yourself?" Grace put her hands on her hips. "You're not in a hotel, Roan. If you share in the benefits of the house, you share in the responsibilities, the least of which is answering the phone so that the few of us who *don't* have to get up can *enjoy* the morning. I don't think that's a very difficult request, is it?"

"Okay, captain," Roan said, flicking her blond hair over her shoulders. "Lay off, I got the message."

Grace pulled two pieces of bread from a bag and popped them into the toaster. Then she poured herself a cup of coffee.

"Listen, Grace," Roan started to say. Her voice was soft and almost nervous sounding. She took a breath and slouched her shoulders, and then her voice came out hard and demanding: "I need some money, you know? I mean, I can't just hang out with no cash at all."

Grace raised her eyebrows. "Money?"

"You said you wanted to help me, so I really need some cash." Roan shot Grace a knowing look. "You don't want me to have to go searching for it, do you?"

Grace crossed the kitchen in a flash and took Roan by the arm, pulling her into the breakfast room.

"Sit," Grace commanded. For a few minutes she studied Roan from across the table. "Okay," Grace said, nodding. "Remember what I just said about sharing in the house responsibilities? If you want some money, why don't you do something around here to earn it." Grace waved her arm behind her. "You can clean up the kitchen, and the two living rooms, on this floor and the one below. If you clean these common areas, *for the household*, I'll give you some spending money."

Roan's jaw had dropped while Grace was speaking. "How much?" was all she managed to squeak out.

"Well," Grace said slowly, "I'll give you three

hours for those three rooms, which is more than enough time. And let's say six dollars an hour, which is a very fair wage. That would make eighteen dollars." Grace paused. "Okay, I'll make it an even twenty."

"Are you kidding?" Roan shrieked. Then she started laughing.

"Why don't you think about it for a minute," Grace snapped. "I'll be right back." She ran upstairs and grabbed her wallet from her purse.

"I'll give it to you right now," Grace said as she returned. She opened her wallet. "Oh," she said, looking surprised. "I was sure I had money in here. Well, listen, I guess I can't give it to you now. But I'll pay you this afternoon."

"Don't you know I can make more than that panhandling?" Roan snapped. "Look, if you want me to work for you, then you're going to have to pay more than slave wages. Unless that's really why you brought me home." Roan narrowed her eyes and stood up. "Maybe all you wanted was a live-in maid! You once asked me what I deserve, and now I'll tell you: It's a lot more than twenty bucks, that's for sure!"

"Listen, Roan," Grace said. "If you aren't interested in my offer, I don't know what else to say. I'm not going to just give you an allowance. To be honest, I don't have to. I'm not your mother. And I also don't think you deserve one. I'm offering you a place here because I want to help you. I want to keep you from making some of the mistakes I made."

Roan sighed and rolled her eyes.

"And being ungrateful was one of them," Grace said icily. She got up from the table. "Let me know when you change your mind, *if* you change your mind, and we'll see what we can work out."

Grace disappeared into the kitchen, and a moment later Roan heard her light step on the staircase heading up to her room. Then she heard the sound of running water.

"Twenty dollars," Roan muttered. "But I'm no damn cleaning lady." She was tired, she'd had another long night. More dreams about her stepfather. Instinctively she hugged herself and ran a hand over her back. With her fingertips, she felt the ridge of scars, the small circular shapes, the old punishment for her various offenses.

"I just wanted to get a little high," she said, whining to herself. "Nothing wrong with wanting to forget about the bad times."

Roan wandered back into the kitchen and looked around for something else to eat. She picked up the bag of bread Grace had left out and started to untwist the wire at the top.

"Well, well, well," a voice said behind her, making her jump. "The little runaway is stealing more bread."

Roan turned slowly to find Tosh leaning in the doorway, eyeing her darkly.

"Aren't you ever satisfied, Roan? I always seem to find you in the kitchen, and you're always hungry. Isn't that right?" Tosh laughed at her and moved closer.

Roan took one step back and studied him. He was wearing boxer shorts, looking like he'd just rolled out of bed.

"See something you like?" he asked.

"Your hair's a mess," Roan said, her voice shaking a little. She was remembering the last time they had met in the kitchen, and the feel of Tosh's mouth against hers. Her heart was beating wildly, but she couldn't tell if she was excited, or afraid, or a little of both.

"What are your troubles today?" Tosh asked her, taking the bread from her limp hands and capturing her wrists in his fingers. "Have another run-in with Mama Grace?"

Roan looked into his dark-blue eyes.

"Sort of," she replied.

"What about this time?"

"Just money."

"What about money?" Tosh said, lifting one of Roan's hands to his lips.

"That I don't have any," Roan said.

"And you want some?"

"She wants me to earn it," Roan corrected.

Tosh lifted her other hand to his mouth and kissed her palm. His blue eyes glittered as he looked at her. "And how does she think you might do that?"

"By cleaning the house." Roan could hardly breathe now. She was definitely having trouble keeping up.

"And you don't want to do it that way, do you?" Tosh said. "So, Roan, how do you want to do it?" he asked. "Earn some money, I mean?"

Roan moved up against him. She could feel his warmth through the sheer nightgown she was wearing. "I thought maybe you could lend some to me?" she suggested.

Tosh's eyes widened and his eyebrows went up. He looked at her quizzically, but with a smirk still at the corners of his mouth. Then he stopped kissing her hands and stepped away from her. Tosh looked at her once again, slowly this time, from her head to her toes and back.

"No, I'm sorry, Roan," he said, laughing deep in his throat. "I don't think I can." He dropped her hands and shrugged as he started to back through the door. "That's never really been my style, you know? And besides," he said, turning from her and walking to the stairs, "you're a dangerous little girl. People could go to jail over you, and I'm just not into that kind of danger." He laughed, and she heard him running up the stairs.

Roan looked at her hands, where he had held them and kissed her. Then she hugged herself again. She thought about what Tosh had said to her before. "Trust me," he'd whispered. Roan had thought he'd be a good ally, someone she could count on to help her. Someone who really liked her. But after the way he played with her this morning, she wasn't so sure.

FOUR

Ten seconds to the right, ten seconds to the left. All day Kate had been scanning the water, scanning the beach. But unfortunately, she hadn't had anything to look at. Nothing to help her pass the time. Not even any gulls. Everyone, including the birds, was off the beach. Everyone but her. Somehow it was a lot harder for her to concentrate. It should have been easier to guard an empty beach. But with no one in the water, no waves, and a gray sky, Kate felt like going to sleep.

"Hey, Quinn," a voice called to her from the bottom of her chair. Kate looked down quickly to see her boss, Luis Salgado. Then her eyes went back to the water.

"Is there a problem?" Kate asked.

"No problem for us," Luis yelled up. "Our job

is easy like this. A problem for the tourist indus-
try. No sun, no fun."

Kate laughed. "You think this job is fun when
the beach is crowded?"

"More fun than sitting in a chair all day feeling
like you want to take a nap."

Kate looked down quickly, wondering if she
had actually been nodding off. Was he trying to
warn her? "I don't nap in the chair," she said
tightly.

"I never suggested you did," Luis said, staring
out at the water. Kate glanced at him again, her
eyes, as always, drawn to the enormous scar that
spread across his side. His trophy for surviving a
great white shark attack. Luis wasn't a man to
mince words. If he'd thought she wasn't paying
attention, he'd have had her out of her chair by
now and halfway home.

"I came by to let you go for the rest of the
day. There's nothing happening here." Kate
grabbed her towel and sun block. She swung
herself down out of the chair and dropped to the
sand beside Luis.

"And of course," Luis said, brushing past her
and pulling himself up onto the chair, "this is not
preferential treatment."

"Of course not, boss," Kate said, smiling. "And
thanks. I promise I won't tell."

Kate threw her towel around her shoulders

34

and pushed a pair of sunglasses onto her nose. The sun wasn't shining, but there was definitely a glare with all the clouds. Though hardly anyone had been on the beach, there were a fair number of people on the boardwalk. It was, after all, the only place to go when the weather was rotten.

Kate herself had always enjoyed the beach when it was cloudy out. She liked to sit on an empty beach, huddled into a sweatshirt, with the sky a blanket of gray clouds, and read or just daydream.

She had actually done that often last summer. She would go to the beach and think about Justin, about whether she and Justin could find a way to save their relationship, or whether they were fated to be star-crossed lovers.

Kate sighed and looked out again at the calm gray sea. To make everything more romantic, she used to imagine her difficulties were large and grand, and wonder how she would continue on without Justin. But of course, now that Justin had died, she no longer felt that way at all. Losing him the way she had seemed exactly the plot of a tragic romance novel. And it hadn't been grand or romantic.

Kate reached the house, but as she was about to go in, she heard a familiar bark from the backyard. "Mooch," Kate called, smiling to herself.

She dropped her towel onto the front stoop and walked around the side of the house. As she reached the patio, she saw Mooch running toward the beach. He stopped and picked up a stick and raced back toward her.

"Wow, Mooch," Kate said. "You sure are ready to play."

Kate bent down with her hand out, waiting for Mooch to bring her the stick. But Mooch didn't come to her. Instead he veered out of her sight and into the trees.

"Hey." Kate stood up and whistled. "Mooch, come here, boy."

Suddenly the stick flew out of the trees toward the beach. Seconds later Mooch bounded after it.

"Who's there?" Kate called. "Who is that?"

Kate saw someone move out of the trees.

"Hey—" Kate started to call again, but the word died in her throat. "Who are you?" The question came out as a whisper, because Kate didn't need to ask. She knew the man standing before her. Only, she had never expected to see him again.

Kate's mouth moved again, though this time no sound came out. Her lips struggled with a word, and Kate felt strong familiar arms around her, as the name caught in her throat: "Justin."

Kate's head spun, and her legs collapsed

below her. But there were the arms holding her up, and a soft familiar voice whispering in her ear, "Kate, it's okay. Katie, it's me."

Justin. Kate could hardly get her mind around it. But it was Justin and those were his arms around her. She shivered with the shock, and the arms quickly fell away. Kate looked up and found herself staring into those eyes, eyes she thought she'd never see again.

"Justin," she spoke, "I can't—" Kate didn't finish. Her arms had gone out to him without her knowing it. Justin pulled her tight against him and his mouth came down on hers. It was the kiss that Kate remembered, the kiss that made her forget who she was and where she was. And now she was forgetting again.

"Justin—" Kate began.

"Kate—" he said.

"I don't understand—" Kate was touching him, pushing at him, still not able to believe he was there.

"I missed you so much." He reached out and stroked her hair.

"But I thought you were dead—"

"I thought so too," Justin said.

"Grace said you'd drowned."

"This is Grace's house, right?" Justin asked, looking over Kate's shoulder. "Is this one of her mother's places?"

"It was, but her mother died." Kate spoke automatically, her mind still trying to catch up with her eyes. "Her mother drowned. You didn't know, of course. Right after Grace came home. After you—"

"And you live here with her?" He looked her up and down, and finally noticed what she was wearing. "And you're guarding now?" he asked.

Kate laughed. "Yeah. I just started. I—" Kate looked down at herself, unsure. "I felt, after I heard about you, that I had to do something. I don't know."

"So that's how much you missed me, huh? Took my job away."

"Actually, you were missed quite a lot." Kate smiled sadly. "We had a memorial on the beach."

Justin took a step backward. "A memorial?" he asked. "To me? What did you say?"

"Lots of things," Kate said, her eyes welling up with the memory. "Luis spoke, and others. They said you were a good guard. A good friend—" Then Kate was crying again, thinking of how she had felt. Remembering that just a week ago, yesterday, even that morning, Justin had been dead. Dead. Gone. Forever.

"I never thought I'd see you again." Kate sobbed into his chest.

"Quiet, quiet, Kate," he whispered, holding her tight. "It's okay, I'm home."

Kate closed her eyes against him and tried to get herself together. Her heart was racing and her head was starting to pound. This would probably be the biggest headache she ever had. Her brain felt like it was working on overdrive, trying to get a handle on what she had just discovered.

"What a day for me to come home," Justin spoke softly. "A cloudy gray day. Perfect for resurrecting the dead."

Kate had just been thinking about gray days, and Justin, and here he was, echoing her own thoughts. But something was nagging her. Something was starting to make her feel sick, and it wasn't the shock of Justin's return. Her heart beat faster, and there was a lump in her throat. She felt herself beginning to choke. There was something else. Something that would be very important now. And then she remembered.

But it wasn't a some*thing*. It was a some*one*. Tosh.

Tosh was the man Kate was in love with now. It seemed strange to say it like that. She loved Tosh now. Justin was supposed to be dead. And in the meantime, Kate had moved on.

Kate pulled away.

"I have to tell you something—" she started to say.

Justin took her hands.

"There's something I have to explain." But Kate didn't get any further.

Behind them they heard the sound of the glass door sliding open. Kate watched Justin look over her shoulder. His eyes lit up and he smiled.

"Hey, Racey," he said, still holding Kate close to him. "You look like you've seen a ghost."

FIVE

Grace's jaw didn't stay dropped for long.

"I would have bet my life I'd seen a ghost," she said. "But then again, Kate has always had her feet pretty firmly planted. If she says you're real, I'll believe her."

Kate turned, her eyes wide. "I'm not sure yet," she said.

Both Grace and Justin laughed. Then Justin went to Grace and wrapped her in his arms. "It's good to see you again, partner. You look better than you did the last time."

Grace smiled and shook her head. "You think I look better?"

There was a bark, and they all turned. Mooch was whining, with the stick at his feet. He trotted over to Justin and pawed his legs.

"Sorry our game was interrupted, Mooch."

Justin scratched his dog on the neck. He looked up at Grace and squeezed her hand. "I was pretty happy to see Mooch here, by the way. I've been too afraid to think about him much. I had no idea whether or not he'd made it." Justin sighed and Grace smiled. "Or you."

"Well, we did," Grace said quickly, her eyes clouding over. "In fact, I think it was Mooch's unmistakably strong scent that kept me from fainting the first two days."

"I'm glad. And thanks for taking care of him."

In silence Kate and Grace watched Justin with Mooch. Neither girl bothered to wipe the tears flowing from her eyes.

"Okay, okay," Grace said. "Enough of the sappy homecoming. Why don't you just come in and let us know exactly how you got home at all."

Justin stood and cocked his elbows. Kate and Grace put their arms through his.

"I thought you'd never ask," he said.

As they came inside, they heard Chelsea's voice floating down from the top of the stairs. "Marta, you look really wiped out. Hope you haven't had the kind of day I've had."

Kate turned to Justin, her hand on his chest. "Oh, Justin, about Chelsea. There's something you don't know—" But Kate's voice was drowned out by the sound of Marta's elevator and the three of them stood still, watching it descend. First the wheels of Marta's chair, and then her feet, her waist, and finally her face, which they watched go white, then red, then white as her eyes flew from Justin to Kate to Grace to Kate and back to Justin.

"Oh my God—"

Justin stepped forward and gently pulled her chair from the lift. "I promise," he said softly, "I'm not a ghost. We just determined it out there on the terrace." He smiled at her and looked quickly over his shoulder. "Ask Kate if you don't believe me. Wait a minute, scratch that." He stood back up, laughing. "You better ask Grace. I think Kate still isn't sure."

In a moment Marta recovered, and called upstairs, "Chelsea, why don't you come down here for a second. I think you'll really want to."

Justin held out while lots of hugs and kisses were exchanged. Then David was called. And Bo and Roan wandered home. Roan was introduced as Grace's "project," and before he could ask, Grace said, "Give her about an hour. You'll recognize exactly why I want to help her to the straight and narrow."

Finally there seemed enough people downstairs for Justin to tell his story. Going through the ordeal once was more than enough for him. Grace and David were on one of the couches.

Chelsea and Kate were on another. Bo and Roan were sitting against a wall, with Mooch between them. And Marta had wheeled herself over next to Justin's chair.

"Okay," he said. "I guess it's time to answer all of your questions."

He sighed and rubbed at his eyes with his hand. Marta reached out and touched him on the arm. Justin turned to her and smiled. Then he spoke.

"First, of course, there was the storm. But I'm sure Grace told you about that. One second there I was on *Kate*." He paused and laughed and looked at Kate. "*Kate* the boat, that is. And the next second I was off her. I hardly even know how it happened, and to tell you the truth, I don't really remember much about being in the water."

Marta reached out and touched Justin on the arm. "You must have been terrified," she said.

"I was," Justin said softly, placing his hand on top of Marta's for a moment. Then he looked at Grace. "And I'm sure I was calling out your name," he said. "I've never been so scared."

"I didn't hear you," Grace whispered, suddenly looking stricken. David had his arm around her, and he squeezed her tightly.

"You couldn't have," Justin said. He cocked his head and stared at her a moment. He saw the

44

creases on her brow, and he leaned toward her. "Grace, it doesn't matter, really. You wouldn't have been able to do anything. We were in the middle of a squall. The most you could do was hang on and try not to drown yourself. Which I'm happy to see you did.

"Anyway," Justin continued, "I was in the water, flailing around, thinking every second that I was drowning." He laughed. "I have no idea how long I managed to stay above water, but just when I felt like I couldn't swim any longer, something hit me on the head."

Everyone was staring at Justin intently, holding their breath.

"A cooler," he said calmly, nodding his head in appreciation. "A good old beach-going Ocean-City–required Styrofoam cooler."

There was silence in the room.

"What did you say?" Kate asked finally.

"A cooler," he repeated. He looked at Grace and shook his head. "You must have held on pretty tight to stay on that boat. Remember we kept that cooler below deck? The boat must have been picked up and shaken out for the cooler to have ended up at sea."

Grace was quiet. Tears were rolling down her face. She tried to speak, but her voice was so low there wasn't a sound. Finally Justin could hear what she was saying.

45

"I threw it in," she said. "I threw it in. I threw everything in. Everything but myself and Mooch."

"All right, Gracie!" Bo yelled, leaping up and crossing the room to his sister. "That means you saved his life, doesn't it? Way to go!"

"Grace," Justin said, "I owe you one, big time."

"I'll tell you what," Grace said, smiling. "Take your little furry friend back, and we'll be just about even."

Grace could feel the grin that was splitting her face. She knew she must look ridiculous. David was nodding and poking her in the side, whispering in her ear, "You see, you see, all the time, you did the right thing." Suddenly Grace realized everyone was staring at her. And there were too many teary eyes, including Justin's. Justin's! Oh God, they were all crying for her. Was it so obvious how she felt?

"I can't take this!" she shouted. "I'm being emotional in front of everybody, and you're all staring at me! Stop this before I start weeping. I swear, nobody has seen me weep and lived to tell about it."

Hands all went to eyes, and the room filled with laughter.

"This looks like quite a party," a voice said, interrupting them. Tosh came down the stairs and walked over to Justin and put out his hand.

"Hi," he said, smiling. "I don't think I've met you yet, but it seems like you're the life of this party. I'm Tosh McCall."

"Justin Garrett," Justin said, taking Tosh's hand. Grace watched Tosh's smile freeze on his face.

"Justin?" Tosh asked slowly. "*The* Justin?"

Justin looked confused for a moment.

"He was at the, you know, the little 'party' we had for you on the beach," David explained.

Tosh walked toward Kate and settled down next to her on the couch. Justin's eyes followed, and when they saw Tosh's arm circle her, they flicked away.

Everyone froze, and the silence and tension in the room seemed to rocket. "Yes, that terrible party," Chelsea finally blurted out. "Well, we'll never have a party like that again, I hope. Anyway, Tosh," she chattered, "Justin was just recounting the story of his survival. And you just missed the part where Grace saves his life. So, umm, Kate, uh—or someone else—will have to fill you in. So," she said, turning to Justin and finally breathing, "then what happened?"

Justin didn't answer for a moment; then he seemed to regain his composure. He nodded and went on: "So I got picked up by a Portuguese fishing boat—"

"Which of course had a broken radio," David guessed.

"Right," Justin said, surprised.

"And of course they were on a long tour," Marta deduced.

"You're right," Justin said. "Two months."

"So you landed in"—Grace paused—"Portugal?"

"And borrowed money from someone, I hope," Chelsea cried.

"The embassy," Justin told her. "How did you know?"

"I think we've all seen this Movie of the Week before," Roan drawled, yawning.

"Hey, can *I* tell this story? Please? I mean I am the one who died. So I borrowed money, flew back, hitchhiked out to O.C., called information for Caywood, and found myself speaking to that lovely young lady," he said, motioning to Roan.

"Lovely yourself," she shot back quickly, and Justin smiled and raised his eyebrow. He glanced over at Grace.

"Don't say it," she snapped. "It's so obvious it hardly needs to be pointed out. I'm like an open book today, I guess." Grace looked over at Roan and asked, "So, has it made you crazy yet how everyone keeps telling you that you're a lot like I was at your age?"

"Yeah," Roan shot back, "but they don't tell

me when I'm gonna get the fancy spread and the flying boyfriend."

"Well, *I* can tell you," Grace said, "you're *not* getting the flying boyfriend."

"So, Justin," Marta said, "where are you staying?"

"Ah, the big question," he answered, glancing at Kate.

Marta looked around. "You know we have these couches—"

"I don't know—"

"Maybe that's not—"

"Really, it might be better—"

Kate, Grace, and Chelsea all started speaking at once.

"Really," Chelsea went on after Kate and Grace fell silent, "it might be better and more comfortable at the apartment across the street with Connor."

"No," Justin said. "I could get a place with one of the lifeguards for a while, I'm sure. I wouldn't want to crowd you two. There's nothing worse than a married couple having to room with someone else. It seems as though it would defeat the purpose—"

"Actually, Justin," Chelsea cut him off, "I have a room here." She paused, and Justin opened his mouth to speak. "Upstairs," she continued. "By myself. So, actually, there's space over there.

49

And I'm sure Connor would enjoy the company."

Justin cocked his head and looked at her quizzically.

"It's a long story," Chelsea said. Her eyes filled with tears. "And I'm a firm believer in one story at a time."

SIX

It was a slow evening at the clinic, which was good because Marta had a lot to think about. So many men appearing from the past in such a short time. The dead returning to life. She was still in shock from seeing Justin that afternoon.

She wasn't surprised when halfway through her shift, she looked up to see Dominic standing in the doorway. His hands were in his pockets, and his eyes were so black she could hardly read them. Marta couldn't tell if his look was challenging or pleading, but she was happy to see him. She told Ming she was taking her break, and rolled outside.

Once on the boardwalk they were silent. Dominic kept his hands deep in his pockets and stared out at the moonlit sea.

"Okay, Dominic," Marta said. "You came to

see me, you can at least speak to me." She smiled up at him as a soft breeze blew her hair around her head.

Dominic stumbled, whispered something, and then coughed to clear his throat. Finally he spoke. "I don't know what to say. I didn't know if you would see me."

"Why wouldn't I see you? Let's go somewhere we can talk, okay?" Marta said. "I have a lot to say."

Dominic nodded. He looked around at the busy boardwalk, the crowds of people wandering by. He reached for her chair.

"Where can I take you?" he asked.

Immediately Marta bristled, and moved a few inches away, out of his grasp. *Cool it,* she thought. *You have more important things to think about tonight than a little independence problem. Let him help,* she told herself.

Marta reached out and caught his hand before it grabbed again for her wheelchair.

"Let's take a stroll up the boardwalk," she suggested. "It gets a lot quieter near my house."

As they moved through the crowd, Marta was comfortable with their silence. She listened to the rhythmic crash of waves hitting the beach, and the happy laughs of people out for a night on the boards.

"So," Marta said after a while. "How is Horror Hall lately?"

Dominic had taken a job playing Dracula and leading tours through the haunted house down on the south end of the boardwalk, near all the amusement rides.

"Well, I scared a lot of people today," he said softly, "but I didn't feel very good about it. Not after last night. Not after scaring you."

"Do I look scared now?" Marta asked, wanting Dominic to look at her. He did, gazing into her eyes for a long moment. Then his eyes moved to her shoulders and chest, and finally to her hands resting on the armrests of her chair.

"No. But you did last night. And you probably should be now."

"Don't tell me what I should be, Dominic. See what I am."

"I see what you are," he snapped. "You're in a wheelchair, for Christ's sake. And I put you there." He frowned, and turned his face away. "I'm sorry," he said softly.

Marta rolled to a stop, and Dominic walked on a few steps before he realized that she was no longer with him. He turned and found her staring at him angrily.

"Listen, you," Marta began. "We need to get something straight. And I think we'd better do it now." Marta felt her heart skip a beat. "I know what I am. I live with it. If I hadn't accepted it, I'd never be who I am today. I don't spend every

53

moment regretting what I could be doing if only I'd never been shot."

"You mean," Dominic corrected, "if only I'd never shot you."

Marta sucked in her breath and sighed heavily.

"It's so hard to look at you and hear you say that at the same time." Marta went to him. "That's because you don't look anything like I imagined you would. That person looked much different to me, in my dreams."

"He must have been a monster," Dominic said.

"But he isn't," Marta insisted. "And that's what counts."

She wheeled over to the edge of the boardwalk and looked out at the sky.

"Dominic," she began. "I had a very long night last night. And it was followed by an incredibly long day." Marta paused and sighed heavily. "You know, one of my friends came back to life. Justin. Remember him? The one we were mourning just a few days ago? Well, he showed up at the house today. Like a ghost. A living ghost. Like you."

Dominic moved to stand next to Marta, but he didn't touch her, and she went on.

"I was so happy to see him alive," she said. "But still, there I was with all this grief that I'd been carrying for him, and I hadn't worked it all out yet. Emotions—deep emotions—don't go away so quickly. Do you understand what I'm saying?"

Marta knew that she was rambling, but she felt so strongly that there was a connection between her discovery of Dominic's past and Justin's return. She hoped that she was making herself clear.

"I feel the same way about you," she continued. "There are feelings I have about the shooting that I could never explain to you. I probably don't understand them all myself. But the past is the past. And you aren't the same person that you were then, so it doesn't seem fair to me to judge you as if you were."

Dominic laid his fingers on her shoulder. They were there just a moment, a light pressure, and then gone.

"Are you sure?" Dominic asked her. "The last thing I want is to lose you now"—he paused—"now that I'm just beginning to know you. But I guess I didn't expect you to be able to forgive me."

"I'm not forgiving you," Marta said quickly, surprising herself. Her words hung in the air between them.

"I don't understand." Dominic's voice was tight, and he stepped away from her.

"What I mean is that I don't have to forgive you. I mean, you aren't the same person who shot me. That person is gone." Marta's voice got stronger and louder as she continued speaking.

"You've changed. I've changed. We don't need that between us. Don't you see?" Marta turned to him and tried to find his eyes in the darkness, but couldn't. He was outlined in the glow of lights from the distant rides. "Don't you see that it doesn't matter what you once did, just like it doesn't matter that I once walked?"

For a moment a thought occurred to her: Am I trying to convince myself of something?

"Come on," she said suddenly, impulsively. "Let's not talk about this anymore." She grabbed his hand and smiled. "I've had so many things to think about lately, I want to do something fun. To escape from my mind a little." But the hand she tugged at was slack. "Dominic, what's wrong?"

"I don't know," he replied. "What you said about me not being the same person. It's true that I don't live the same life that I once did, but I'm still the same person, Marta—"

"No!" Marta snapped. She didn't want to hear this. "No, Dominic, you're not the same person. Believe me."

She wheeled past him and turned, forcing him to face her. She wanted to see his face in the light. "Look," she said quickly. "Do you want to be with me or not?"

"Very much," Dominic replied slowly.

"Okay, then. Let's go somewhere."

Dominic sighed and came over to her.

"As long as you're not thinking of another race." He smiled.

"As a matter of fact, I do feel like a sprint." Dominic's smile froze, and Marta laughed. "But I'll take a scare instead."

"Ahhh," he said slowly, and hunched over. Dominic put on his best Dracula smile and spoke in a low, creepy voice. "The lady vants a scare. This vay to Horror Hall, madam. This vay, please."

Marta laughed, and followed him as he started down the boardwalk, bent over and dragging his foot behind him. Every few steps he turned to look back at her. "Am I scaring you yet?" he asked.

When they got to Horror Hall, Marta looked up at the imposing black facade. The walls were painted with ghoulish scenes of monsters and headless bodies dripping blood.

"You know," Marta said, "I've never actually been in here before."

"Really?" Dominic seemed surprised. "Are you sure you want to do this, Marta? I mean, some of it is really silly, but some of it can be frightening."

"What are you saying?" Marta asked. "You think I can't take care of myself? It's a little late for you to worry about protecting me, isn't it?"

Dominic flinched as if she had hit him.

"Look," Marta said, reaching out to him. "I'm sorry. I didn't mean that. But really, you have to stop being so concerned about me. Come on," she said. "Let's go in."

"But, Marta," Dominic began, "I should warn you about—"

"Dominic, stop!" Marta said. "Really. Just stop." She rolled herself to the front door and Dominic followed, and the man taking tickets, a tall green version of Frankenstein's monster, smiled at Dominic and Marta and let them in.

Inside, they were immediately plunged into darkness. Marta jumped at the change and shivered. Come on, she said to herself. It's just a corny haunted house.

But the hallway was impossibly black, and she couldn't see Dominic anywhere, she could only feel bodies pushing up against her and trying to move around her. Marta heard people muttering as they ran into her chair. She couldn't seem to get out of anyone's way as the hallway turned back and forth at sharp angles, and she was getting nervous. When was the first scare coming? she wondered, her hands gripping the wheels of her chair in anticipation.

Someone touched her on the shoulder and she screamed. At the same time there was a loud screeching noise as something fell from the ceiling. Marta heard it, and felt something heavy and wet brush against her arm. All around her people were shrieking and pushing. She was trapped with no room to maneuver her chair. Someone had grabbed her chair, and as they turned another corner, a figure in white leapt out from behind a dark curtain. Marta was sure she saw a knife in the flash of electric blue light, and she tried to move but she was pinned.

Before she could stop herself, she was screaming uncontrollably. She felt the bodies moving away from her, and finally she was able to grip the wheels of her chair and turn around.

"What is it?" voices were saying.

"What's wrong with her?"

"She's freaking out."

"Is someone hurt?"

"Get back, give her room."

"She shouldn't be in here in that chair—"

"She's just in the way."

Suddenly Marta felt herself being lifted from her chair and carried through the darkness. In moments she burst out the front door, and Frankenstein was looking at her, asking what had happened. Marta was clutching on to the arms of her savior, and she gazed up to find Dominic's face twisted with concern, and with something else. Fear.

"Put me down here," Marta said tightly, trying to get back her breath. Gently Dominic placed her on a bench right outside.

"Marta," Dominic began, "what happened—"

But Marta was quick to answer, cutting him off before he could ask any more. "Just do me a favor," she said icily. "Please. Get my damn chair so I can get home."

Dominic walked her home in silence. When they got to the front door of her house, he touched her lightly on the arm, and she jumped.

"I'm sorry," he said, his dark eyes pained.

"It's okay," Marta answered, fishing for her keys. "It has nothing to do with you," she said.

As she closed the door behind her, Marta wondered who she was trying to reassure— Dominic or herself.

SEVEN

Roan was having trouble focusing. Light was coming from her window, though she knew it was the middle of the night.

"Must be the stars," she whispered. "How lucky for the stars. They can go out every night. But not me."

Roan was on her bed, leaning against the wall. She hadn't even tried to sleep, because she knew she wouldn't have been able to. She could always tell if a night would be full of frightening dreams. And so she usually stayed awake to avoid them.

"Easier to fight bad memories awake, that's the truth." Roan was talking to herself softly and rocking back and forth. "And easier to stay awake with a friend," she said, clutching tightly the bottle she was drinking from.

"I just don't have too many friends," she explained. "That's why I need you."

The bottle didn't answer, but she knew it understood.

"I can't go out, I can never go out, no one ever lets me out," she chanted.

Roan took a drink and peered out the window. She tried to find the moon. It was a faint shiny blur through her half-closed eyes.

She leaned her head back, and her eyes closed all the way. In an instant, she was back home. Everything was the same: the tiny kitchen whose counter and sink were strewn with empty brown beer bottles; the cramped living room, a couch with stained and sunken cushions; the chipped and peeling paint on the walls and ceilings; the small black-and-white TV, continually on.

Roan wandered through the house. She went to her room, but it was empty. "Good," she said out loud. "I'm still gone."

She heard a heavy step behind her and she tensed.

"You're gone?" the deep voice asked. "I thought I told you never to leave. I thought I told you to stay and help your mama. You know you're not supposed to go anywhere unless I say you can."

Then Roan was running through the house, trying to get away, screaming for her mother to help her.

"Your mama won't say nothing," the voice said, panting. "She wants me to take care of you. She knows you need discipline."

Roan felt the strong arm grab her and she was thrown onto the floor. "Don't you go screaming for your mama like that, girl. You shouldn't bother her like that. She needs peace and quiet, and you need to learn to be a quiet girl."

Roan felt her stomach tighten into knots.

"I'm going to teach you to be quiet, girl."

Roan tasted blood in her mouth as she bit down hard on her cheeks, trying not to scream. She closed her eyes, waiting for the pain to come.

Roan jerked awake in silence. Her teeth were clamped together and the metallic taste of blood was on her tongue. She was breathing rapidly through her nose. *Not home,* her mind screamed. *You're not home. It was only a dream, that's all.*

Roan grabbed the bottle and raised it. The alcohol stung her where she'd bitten her cheeks. She wrapped her arms around herself and began rocking.

"I'm gone, I'm gone, I'm gone," she whispered. "And you can't touch me anymore."

Marta was dreaming. There it was again, the total darkness. Something was grabbing at her arms, holding her down so that she couldn't get away, and Marta was twisting, twisting, her throat tight. Just about to scream, Don't touch me!

Her eyes snapped open. She felt a flash of terror, not knowing where she was. And then she was awake, covered in sweat and tangled in her sheets.

What had happened to her? All night every time she closed her eyes she ended up at Horror Hall. It had been hours since Dominic had brought her home, and she was still frightened.

What a stupid thing she'd done! There had been so many people there. The darkness had made it worse, and when the shrieking began, and that wet . . . whatever, had hit her, and the man with the knife had jumped out—well, she had just lost control.

She'd felt the old kind of paralyzing feeling. Like she'd felt back in the hospital right after the accident, when there was nothing she could do, nowhere she could go. She had been helpless.

Marta couldn't get Dominic's face out of her mind; his dark black eyes, staring at her from the boardwalk when she and Grace had first seen him. And there was the other face. The blue face of the snake on his chest.

Her room disappeared from around her, and Marta could no longer hear the soft sound of the ocean. Instead she heard the low hum of machinery and the beep of the life-support system and monitor she had been on for so long after the accident.

That had been the real Horror Hall. The minutes and hours and days that dragged by while she watched the ceiling of a hospital room. She did nothing for weeks but follow the course of a crack in the paint and think about how she would never walk again. Think of all the things she would never be able to do again.

Marta remembered the endless hours in rehab. She couldn't keep it from her mind now: the activity room, with the weights and the parallel bars where she tried to hold herself up. The strangers who were so intimate with her then, who pulled off her pants for her, cleaned her, bathed her, before she could do any of it on her own. The ones who stood there, chatting to each other while they rubbed and massaged her lifeless legs to keep the blood pumping through them. And so many people looking at her, always looking at her with sad and sorry eyes.

Marta lay still, thinking of it all. All the days of anger. All the days of depression and fear. All the days of watching her father standing over her, watching the hope in his eyes that maybe, just maybe, she would get better.

In the background of every memory were two faces. One, the blue snake head holding a skull between its fangs. The other a dark-haired man with black eyes. And as Marta remembered more and more, the two faces began to merge into one.

Upstairs Chelsea was having trouble with the face. She was in bed, bent over her sketch pad. Drawing always soothed her when she was anxious, and for some reason tonight she was too anxious to sleep. She was trying to draw a picture of Steve, her coworker at The Face Place. He'd told her if he ever did her portrait he would draw a bird with a heavy chain around its neck.

Well, he sure wasn't any more free than she was. A gay son in an upright political family. She was sketching him now, head and shoulders peeking out from behind a screen while dark shadowy figures looked down at him from the background.

"Hmmm," she said to herself. "You're not being too heavy-handed on the metaphor, are you, Chels?

"No," she answered. "Ridiculous. Too metaphorical? What does she know? Don't listen to her, you're the artist."

Chelsea continued to work on the drawing as her mind drifted. When she focused again, the face behind the screen had freckles and distinctively reddish hair.

Chelsea frowned and pushed the pad off her

lap. Her pencils fell to the floor by the bed.

"How dare you, you lowlife Irish criminal," she hissed at the picture that now looked suspiciously like a black-skinned Connor. "Sneaking into my picture when I'm not thinking about you. Do you hear me?" she said loudly, pointing a finger at the drawing. "I'm not thinking about you."

Chelsea leaned back and thought of the house they'd lived in last summer. She and Connor had lived right next door to each other. They had shared a wall, and she could hear his every movement. She had listened to the squeak of his bedsprings and the rustle of his sheets. And she knew he had listened to her.

"Come on, Chelsea," she said. "What are you doing lying here getting yourself all hot and bothered? There's more than a wall between you now." She sighed. "There's a wall, a yard, a street, a yard, and another wall." But she knew she couldn't sleep. She was just too lonely.

Chelsea got up and wrapped herself in a brightly patterned sarong. She went to the only window and stood staring at her unfortunate view. The old Victorian house was directly across the street. Chelsea could see the tiny balcony of Connor's apartment on the second floor. The tiny balcony that used to be her tiny balcony too. The soft glow of a yellow light fell from the window and glinted on the railing. Chelsea saw a shadow pass by the curtains, and she ducked her head back into her own room as a dark figure stepped out onto the balcony.

"Well, I hope you're having as much trouble sleeping as I am," Chelsea said, her head leaning back against her wall, her heart beating rapidly. "Though somehow," she whispered sadly, wiping a tear from her eye, "it doesn't make me feel any better."

"Oh, Mooch," Justin moaned, pushing the dog off the couch. "Are you going to keep me up all night, boy? I know you miss me, but I've got to get some sleep."

Justin listened to the steady snoring coming from the bedroom.

"Go on, Mooch, go wake up Connor. Sounds to me like he's sleeping much too well." Justin got up from the couch and led the dog to the bedroom door. He opened it and pushed Mooch inside. The snoring stopped, and Justin put his ear against the door.

"Mmm, Chels, you came back to me, lass." Justin heard the bedsprings shift and the sheets rustle. Then, "Damn," the Irish voice piped. "Ack, ugh, what the—"

There was a loud thump and Mooch came slinking out the door. A moment later Connor emerged, red hair on end, a sheet wrapped around his middle. His eyes were on fire.

"Garret!" he screeched, his face red. "I'm happy to have you back, mate, but if you want to stay alive, keep that scruffy rag out of my bed, right?"

Connor sank down into a chair and scratched his head. "Scared the hell out of me, he did. Couldn't think what I'd gone and done."

Justin sat on the couch opposite him. "Actually," he said, "you thought it was Chelsea."

Connor's eyes darkened and he looked away. "Ahh," he said softly. "So I did." He was quiet a moment and then he sat up quickly. "But don't tell her I mistook her for a dog, okay? 'Cause you know, then I'll never get her back." Connor's laugh was forced, but Justin joined him.

Connor got up and went to the kitchen. He came back with two open bottles of Guinness.

"Join me for one?" Connor said, passing a bottle to Justin. "You know how we Irish hate to drink alone."

They drank in silence for a while.

"Hey now, what am I thinking?" Connor finally said. "Here we are, two handsome bachelors awake in a city of sin. It's not that late, is it? There's sure to be some pretty girls out needing assistance from fine gentlemen like ourselves. I always wanted to follow around a lifeguard. You can revive 'em, and I'll try to make 'em pass out again." Connor took a swig from his beer, though he made no move at all to get up. "Come on now, what do you say?"

Justin faced the window. "I just came back to life myself," he said. "I don't know if I'm ready to save anyone else yet."

"Hmmm, yeah," Connor said. "Must have been quite a shock, coming back? What with Kate and that new guy of hers."

Justin closed his eyes a moment. "A shock," he said. "Yes, I guess it was. Pretty stupid of me, but I just kept thinking, If only I can make it back to O.C., everything will be fine." He paused. "Then I'll know I'm really saved."

"It's not that stupid," Connor said glumly. "That's what we came back for. Back to Ocean City and all the bickering will stop. Back to Ocean City, where we don't have to worry every minute about our futures and who shopped last and who cleaned the dishes and who still hasn't found a job. Well," Connor said sadly, looking around, "here we are. Only, we aren't 'we' anymore, are we?"

Justin walked out onto the tiny balcony and smelled the night air. He could hear the waves rolling onto the beach. He leaned over the railing and could just make out the dark blackness of the sea.

Had he been a fool, thinking Kate would be here for him? What had he expected? They'd all thought he was dead. They'd even buried him on the beach, he'd been told. What would have been the point of her waiting for a dead person? It only would have meant she wasn't getting on with her life, and he wouldn't have wanted that. Would he?

He shook his head to clear it. That wasn't the question anymore, he told himself. It didn't matter what he'd done, or what she'd done. He couldn't change any of that. The real question was, What could he do now?

Over at Grace's he could see that a few windows glowed with dim light. He wondered if one of them was Kate's. He hoped not. If she was awake at this hour, there was probably only one reason, and he pushed it from his mind as quickly as possible. But then again, it wasn't any better to imagine her asleep. Awake or asleep, she was in her bed with someone else.

He sighed and looked toward the darkness of the ocean. "You can't come home again."

Justin walked inside from the balcony. As he walked past Connor, he put his half-finished bottle on the coffee table.

"I'm never going to sleep tonight," he said as he went to the door. "I'll see you in the morning."

"Where are you going?" Connor asked listlessly.

"Just for a swim. I really need to cool off," Justin said, closing the door on his way out.

EIGHT

Kate was so close to the edge of the bed, she was almost out of it. She was tense, and she wasn't sleeping. Somehow she just couldn't close her eyes. She listened for the breathing behind her and was glad to hear that it was still steady.

All night she had been avoiding Tosh's body. It was a pretty hard thing to avoid someone you were sleeping with. She was exhausted from all the nighttime gymnastics. Every time Tosh had rolled over, stretched out, or reached for her, she had managed to stay just out of his grasp. Kate didn't know exactly why she was doing it. She felt terrible about it, actually. For the first time since she'd started seeing Tosh, she was embarrassed and uncomfortable to be in bed with him. Up until last night they had done little more than lie next to one another while they slept, and it

73

had always been comfortable. But now, suddenly, it felt as though something was wrong.

When they'd finally come to her room earlier, Tosh had wanted to talk.

"Kate," he'd whispered in the darkness. "You must be feeling very confused right now."

"No," she'd answered. "I'm fine, really."

"I'm here to help, you know," he'd said, reaching out to her under the covers. Kate had flinched, though she hadn't meant to.

"Tosh, please," Kate had pleaded. "It's been a long day. For both of us. I really can't talk about it tonight. Please," she'd said while she leaned over and kissed him quickly. "I just need to sleep now."

Tosh had sighed and rolled over. Kate had closed her eyes, but sleep was the last thing that came to her.

Now she was so far over on the bed, she really had nowhere left to go but the floor.

This is crazy, she thought. *You've got to get out of here and do something to relax.*

Quietly Kate slid off the edge of the mattress. She turned and watched the dark shape that was Tosh, waiting to see if she'd woken him with her movements. When she was sure that he was still asleep, she moved away from the bed and went to the dresser. Careful not to make noise, she pulled open one of the drawers and felt around for her bathing suit. She put it on quickly, along with a T-shirt, grabbed a towel from her chair, and slipped soundlessly from the room.

Outside the house the air was warm. It was also bright. It was that time of night, well past midnight, when the sky turned from black to a deep, almost pale blue. It had always amazed Kate how the sky changed so during the night. It would get darker again, she knew, from three to six, just before sunrise. But now there was enough light for her to see. Kate wandered past the terrace and onto the sand. The sea was dark before her, and Kate sucked in her breath.

The sight of the ocean at night always awed her. It was so immense. So dark. Disappearing at its edges into the night sky. She couldn't see the waves yet, but she could hear them. The sand was cool beneath her feet. Kate stripped off her shirt and shorts and walked to the water's edge. The waves rolled over her feet. The water was unusually warm.

"Kate?"

She jumped at the sound of her name and turned to find a figure standing by her clothes.

"I thought that was you," he said. "I couldn't imagine it would be anyone else."

"Justin," his name slipped from her throat.

He grunted, and she saw his arm go to his head. She couldn't see it clearly, but she knew the gesture so well. He was running his fingers through his hair. He was nervous.

He laughed. "I came for a swim. Great minds think alike, wouldn't you say?"

"Is that what we are?" Kate asked. "Great minds?"

Justin walked over and stood beside her in the water. "You are, that's for sure. But I don't believe anymore I'm as smart as I liked to think I was. There's one or two things I wasn't smart enough to figure on."

Kate turned away, knowing what he meant but having no answer for him.

"So," he finally said. "Join me for a swim? For old times' sake?" Justin walked past her and dove into the dark waves.

Well, Kate, she asked herself, *that's what you came for, isn't it?* And before she could question herself any further, she followed.

The cool seawater closed around her as she plunged in. When she came up, she felt suspended, invisible. She heard the sound of Justin stroking through the waves. She could barely see him, a pale spot in the darkness, but she lowered her head and swam toward the noise. Soon they were side by side. Guarding had made her a strong swimmer. Their strokes were equal as they cut through the ocean toward the black horizon.

Finally, far from shore, they stopped. Treading water, Kate watched Justin's head bobbing near her. She felt the wake from his kicking legs beat against her body. He swam closer, and she would have sworn the water near her grew warmer.

Justin floated behind her and took her body in his arms, his strong legs kicking harder to keep them both afloat. Kate felt her body melting on the outside, but inside, her blood was coursing, boiling. With her eyes open she saw only the black waves and the dark sky. Stars glittered above her. The hard familiar body held her. It was like a dream, this feeling. And she almost, almost convinced herself that she could escape. Escape history. Escape the past. Escape the present. Almost.

She pulled away abruptly and dove. Salt stung her eyes. When she surfaced, she turned toward Justin.

"We need to go back," she said.

"Yep," he answered.

"To shore. That's what I meant."

"Uh-huh, I know." Kate watched as he slipped below the water. She reached out a hand, frightened.

"Justin—"

But then she saw him, already speeding back to the beach. She put her head down and followed once more.

When she came out of the water, he was sitting on the sand next to her clothes, wrapped in her towel. Kate dropped down next to him, and he pulled the towel around her shoulders.

"Justin," she began, hardly knowing what she would say. "I never thought I would see you again. You know that."

"You don't have to excuse yourself for living, Kate. It's my mistake. I was so happy to be alive, I never stopped to think what could happen while I was gone."

"You know Tosh isn't the only thing between us," Kate pointed out. "He's just the most obvious. We've been through this twice before, without you dying, and without Tosh."

"There was a reason we kept trying," Justin said softly. "Wasn't there?"

"And anyway, what do you think would happen at the end of the summer?" Kate demanded, not ready to answer his question. "What could be different now? Three times lucky? We need more than that. I'm still in school and I'm going back in the fall. And what will you be doing then?"

Justin looked away. "I don't know."

"We were drifting, Justin," Kate said, turning to him. "Don't you see?" She knew she was pleading, though she didn't know why. "Even last summer, at the end, before you ever left, we were drifting." Kate reached out and put her hand on his arm. Justin stared at her in the dim light. "Love wasn't enough, Justin," she said softly. "Somehow, for us, it wasn't enough."

"No," he said, leaning toward her. "You're wrong, Kate." His head dipped and he put his lips against her ear. "I'm glad Grace never heard me call for help, because I never called for her. I called for you. When I was there, in the water, and I thought I was going to die, everything fell away—the boat, Grace, Mooch, my whole life— except for you. You were the only thing I saw, Kate. The only thing I couldn't leave. The thought of dying didn't frighten me. But the thought of losing you did."

Justin slipped his arm beneath Kate's towel and pulled her body against him. His lips hovered above hers.

"Love was enough for me, Kate," he whispered. "It was always enough for me."

And then he stopped talking.

Kate's world fell away as their lips met. Her body responded on its own. She was grabbing at him, running her hands everywhere—his neck, his chest—touching the skin she thought she'd never caress again.

She kissed his throat, and he slipped one hand below her suit. His fingers moved lightly along her back, her shoulders, her stomach.

"Oh my God." Kate suddenly pulled away, grabbed her clothes, and stood. "Justin, I can't do this. What about Tosh? I won't do this behind his back."

Kate began backing away, clutching her towel in front of her. Justin didn't move. He just sat there on the beach, staring up at her. The last thing she heard was his voice saying sadly, full of disappointment, "I know you won't, Kate. But that doesn't stop me from loving you."

NINE

"Ahh, here we are. And there you are. Grace Caywood, proprietress. Off to survey your domain." David parked Grace's BMW in a small lot at the southernmost end of the boardwalk. He leaned back with his arms behind his head and gazed at his passenger.

"You are the most beautiful landowner this poor desolate stretch of beach has ever seen."

Grace had her dark hair pulled up into what she called her "imposing and professional" look.

"A woman with a bun always makes me shudder," she had said that morning.

Grace was wearing a cropped linen jacket and matching shorts, fashionable but respectable. She was carrying a smart leather briefcase.

"Don't you think this is a little too much?" she'd asked David when he'd given it to her as a present for her new role as a civic-minded member of the business community. "I own a few beach stands," she'd said. "It's not like I'm opening a hotel."

"Maybe not yet," David had said. "In any case, you may not think so, but appearances do matter when you're an employer. They may only be beach stands, but if you act like a kid, then the kids you hire won't take you seriously. You don't need to be a hard-ass, but you need for them to see you're in control."

And, of course, David had been right. The way Grace looked had mattered. A lot. When she'd started hiring, she lost a good number of people, mostly eighteen- and nineteen-year-old young men who didn't feel comfortable working for a woman their age. Particularly a woman in a bikini. They'd spent all their interviewing time trying to get her out on a date. And in her first week, she'd fired a few girls with attitude problems who had made the mistake of thinking that Grace wasn't serious enough to reprimand them for being late.

Now she was off on her morning rounds, to check on her six stands and make sure that they were open and that everyone had shown up for work. Grace had rented all of her beach stands next to each other on what she knew was the busiest stretch of beach along the two-mile boardwalk.

Grace leaned over and gave David a kiss.

"Thanks for the ride, flyboy," she said. "Now don't get lost in any clouds with those students of yours."

"Don't worry," he answered her, holding her chin in his hand. "You're the only student that's ever flown me to the moon."

Grace pulled away from him. "For an older man, that's one of the worst lines I've ever heard," Grace snorted.

"Ah, yes." David sighed, smiling, and started the engine. "So true, so true."

Chelsea was on the boardwalk with her sketch pads. Her boss, Maurice, had let her off from The Face Place this morning for a new assignment.

"I do the funny pictures," he'd said. "And believe me, with this crowd I love to do them."

Chelsea knew he wasn't kidding. Maurice was the greatest caricaturist she'd ever seen.

"And you three," he'd said to Steve, Sophie, and Chelsea, "do the portraits. You make everyone look just the way they want to look, and perhaps not always how they really do look. That's another kind of magic."

Maurice gestured around the small shop.

"But I'd like to see some other kinds of drawings in here. I'm getting a little tired of faces. I'm commissioning some real art from you art students. Who wants to go out and work with the people?"

Chelsea had been the first to speak, anxious to be outside on such a beautiful day, and so Maurice had sent her "into the wild crowd," as he called it, to sketch "the seething populace."

Well, they're not exactly seething, Chelsea thought as she sat on a bench and scouted the crowd on the boardwalk. *But they're really horribly dressed.*

She spotted a particularly interesting couple and began drawing them. The heavy woman was wearing an enormous gold lamé swimsuit with a loose matching wrap. Yards of black chiffon wound sarong-style around her waist. She teetered on slinky black heels, and a diamond necklace glinted from her throat. Her husband was wearing what looked like a silk dressing gown. Chelsea drew the couple with clear, bold strokes. Then she surrounded them with abstract images of the half-naked hardbodies that sauntered past them on the boardwalk, beautiful and lithe young men and women, careless and unaffected. In the background she sketched the souvenir stands with their cartoon signs and tacky wares.

"That's a very intelligent and interesting vision you have there," a voice said from over her shoulder.

Chelsea stopped drawing and held out her

sketch pad, looking at it with her head cocked.

"I think you've really captured them." A dark-skinned hand came into view and pointed at the older couple in the center. "Just a little out of place, perhaps?"

Chelsea laughed. "Or not out of place at all," she replied. "In this place, the fact that they stand out means they fit in just fine."

"A good dose of irony. And reality. I like your style."

Chelsea turned to find herself looking at a very handsome African-American man wearing light khakis and a short-sleeve denim shirt. She quickly judged him to be in his late twenties.

"Paul Hagen," he said, extending his hand.

"Chelsea Lennox," she replied.

"I'm pleased to meet you, Chelsea. And I hope I haven't interrupted. I've been watching you draw for a while."

"Well," Chelsea said. "I hope you don't take this the wrong way, but I really hadn't noticed."

Paul laughed and flashed his very white and very straight teeth.

"No," he agreed, "I see that you didn't. But I'm glad. I wouldn't have wanted to stop that." He pointed to her sketch pad. "I'm a true aficionado of the arts."

"I'm going to assume that means you like them."

"Yes." He laughed again. "It certainly does mean I like them. I like the arts." He paused and looked at her closely. "And I especially like the artists."

Chelsea felt herself blushing. This Paul Hagen was very handsome. And very charming. Chelsea hadn't had a conversation like this in a long while. A conversation that made her feel happy and talented. And sexy.

"So, Chelsea Lennox, artist."

Chelsea chuckled at the way he said that. Then Paul leaned forward and took her hand.

"I'm starving," he said. "Perhaps you can sketch me lunch? Or you can let me take you out for a real one."

This is a nice man, Chelsea thought. The first nice man I've talked to in a while. What crime would it be to go out for lunch with a nice man who made her laugh? Especially a nice man who was so attractive.

"I'd love to," Chelsea finally answered, smiling up at Paul's face. "Let *you* take *me* out to lunch, I mean."

"I like that smile," Paul said. "You light up when you smile, Chelsea. I hope you'll keep doing so."

"Well, that's your job for the afternoon," she shot back at him. "To keep me smiling."

And to help me have a little fun, she said silently. *Because I'm sure that's what Connor is doing. Having plenty of his own fun.*

"I don't know anyway who are you, you think, but hungry at least, because in your mouth this whole beach you see?"

Connor looked at the enormous blond hard oily thing in front of him. This guy must lift weights with his lips, Connor thought. Almost certainly inhuman.

"What did he just say?" Connor cried. "I'll admit it, he's got me baffled."

"I don't know who you think you are," Grace translated, "but you're about to eat this beach."

"Oh," Connor said. "Thanks, Grace."

He turned back to the bodybuilder. "Who do I think I am?" Connor said in a high-pitched voice. "Why, I'm Prince Charming come to rescue the damsels in distress." He gave the muscle-bound nightmare a leering look. "And you must be the one-eyed ogre."

"Connor, don't—" Grace stepped forward, putting her hand on Connor's arm. "Just forget it," she said.

"Yah, Prince, you hear," said the hulkster. "You forget now. Go home and a small green man, where you belong to play with."

"Go back home where you belong," Grace said slowly, "and find a leprechaun to play with."

87

The hulkster stood with his hands on his hips, grinning broadly, the muscles rippling across his chest and arms.

"That was a low blow," Connor hissed.

"Look, wait a minute," Grace said angrily, stamping her foot uselessly in the sand. "This situation has nothing to do with you men." She looked at Connor. "Either of you, although believe me, I appreciate the moral support."

Grace turned to Judy. Judy was huddled against the beach stand, looking meek and guilty.

"Judy," Grace said. "You have a job now. That means responsibility. You can't just take off with your boyfriend whenever you want." The hulkster growled. Grace shot him a nasty look. "No matter how big he is," she said sternly. "This is the third time you haven't been here when I've stopped by. If this stand doesn't earn any money, I'll close it. And then I'll have to fire you. So if I'm going to pay for your work, then dammit, work for me!"

Judy opened her mouth to speak, but then she looked over at her boyfriend, who was glaring at Grace.

"Hans?" Judy asked tentatively. "I can't go with you to the gym, okay?"

"No!" he yelped. "Not okay."

Hans moved toward Grace from the front, and Connor moved up behind her.

"Wait a minute," Grace said, her eyes wide. "Cut this macho crap right now."

"I cut you," Hans said. "Judy done here. No more work for you. Bad pay, and in the chair, no clothes on all day, and read book, naked women on top. I don't like it."

Connor turned to Judy and asked sincerely, "And how do you feel?"

"She feels same," Hans demanded. "Judy, come now with me. No more job reading naked in chair."

Judy reached into the beach stand and grabbed her bag and her sandals.

"Judy," Grace asked. "You're quitting? Just like that?"

"I'm sorry, Grace, but I guess I have to."

She and the hulkster turned and walked away.

After a moment Grace and Connor both shook their heads.

"Wow," they said at the same time.

"Did we just go through a time warp?" Connor asked. "I can't believe that guy is for real. They don't grow them like that at home."

"Most definitely *Planet of the Apes*," Grace agreed. "Anyway," she said, hooking her arm through Connor's, "thanks for your support. You were ready to risk life and limb for me. I'm touched."

"Actually, it was just reporter's instinct. When

I saw that monstrosity yelling at you, I thought there might be a good story in it."

Grace laughed. "You mean a good human-interest story?"

"No," Connor said, grinning. "More like 'Murder on the Beach'!"

"Well," Grace said, "I came away unscathed. Sorry to disappoint you."

"No matter," Connor answered. "There's always next time."

"Thanks a lot for the good thoughts, Connor. I'll keep it in mind next time I see you."

Connor raised his eyebrows and looked hurt. Then he put his hand to his chest and began stumbling around in the sand.

"That's it, I knew it," he moaned. "I've become a pariah. No one loves me anymore. Rejected by all—my friends and family turning on me—I'll just wander the beach, looking for love."

"All right, Shakespeare. Why don't we just wander for ice cream instead? I owe you one," Grace said, laughing as they started for the boardwalk. "And then I'm going to head home and try to solve my employee problem."

Grace pulled out her wallet and looked inside.

"Oops," she said. "Connor? You know the ice cream I said I owed you?"

"Are you telling me that the land baroness is broke?" Connor asked.

"She didn't think she was," Grace replied, shaking her head and looking into her empty wallet. "But the evidence would appear to show otherwise."

"Okay." Connor nodded. "I get it. I save your life, and I still get stuck with the tab."

"So," Paul said, "I'd like to proposition you, Chelsea. What do you think about that?"

Chelsea almost choked on her seafood salad.

Her face was so hot, she was afraid her hair would start burning. She coughed, and then she managed to swallow.

"I'd say I better hear it before I say any more," she finally squeaked out.

Paul had taken her to Dockside's, a restaurant on the bay that had a great view of the water from its patio. Their green-and-white table umbrella swayed in the breeze.

Paul laughed heartily. "Well, this proposition isn't the kind I think you think it is." He smiled warmly and then added, "After you answer, though, maybe I can come up with another."

He poured more iced tea into his glass from the pitcher on the table.

"This proposition is for a job," he said. "I'm in advertising, by the way. And I have a small local branch office here in O.C. that I'm trying to staff right now. And," he said, looking at her pointedly,

"I'm looking for some local talent. Some artists."

"For what kind of work?" Chelsea asked.

"Oh, laughing crabs and happy clams, most likely. Restaurant ads mainly. And anything else you can think of that would be advertised here in O.C."

"Like suntan lotion?" she asked.

"Or bikinis," Paul said.

"Or Rollerblades?"

"Or bikinis."

Chelsea laughed. "Hmm," she said. "I'm sure there's something I'm missing. Let's see. Beach. Water. Swimming." She tapped her forehead with her finger. "Swimwear? I got it," She said thoughtfully. "Bikinis!"

"Great idea," Paul said. "Feel free to use yourself as a model."

"Oh, I doubt my body would sell a bikini," Chelsea said.

"Oh, I'd have to disagree," Paul said, looking at her intently. "But anyway, I'm serious about the work, Chelsea. I think you're very talented. You've got a quirky eye and a great sense of humor."

"Well," she said.

"Listen, Chelsea, I know what you're thinking. I definitely find you attractive, and in fact, I'd love it if I could spend some more time with you. I was thinking about dinner tonight, actually. But don't forget, I've also seen you work. And while I watched you draw, all I saw was the back of your head. That's when I decided to offer you a job." Paul smiled.

"Chelsea, I'm offering you a job, and I'm offering you a date. They're two separate offers. Business is business, and I believe you'd be good for my business. You have a job—if you want it. And I'll have a date tonight—but only if you want that, too."

Chelsea watched two water-skiers on the bay. They were being pulled by the same little boat, but it looked as though they refused to just ski along side by side. They kept crossing back and forth in front of each other, almost tangling their towlines, and then shooting out alongside the boat to ride the bumpy wake. Two people connected to the same speeding boat trying to do two completely different things.

She knew that she and Connor were still connected. But their marriage had started feeling like the speeding boat; it was dragging them along behind, but they weren't ready to go in the same direction. And like the water-skiers, she wondered whether one of them would have to break free if they were to keep from crashing.

Advertising. A new job. A new direction. Chelsea looked at Paul. "I'll take it," she said. "Both the job and the dinner."

TEN

Grace stood on the deck of the house, the sandy beach spreading before her to the ocean. A thick cloud of gulls swarmed over an invisible school of fish. She looked along the warm white beach and out at the surf and smiled.

"I'll admit it," Grace said, "this house has a fantastic view."

"It's a little thin on men up here, though." Roan lay back, her eyes closed against the sun. She was stretched out in a beach chair, wearing, Grace thought, a *very* skimpy bikini. But after a second look, Grace had to admit that the bikini wasn't any tinier than the ones she habitually wore. *It must be this motherly instinct I've been feeling lately,* Grace said to herself.

On the deck below Roan's chair were a couple of tubes of suntan lotion. Grace recognized them instantly.

"It looks as though my cabinet is a little thin on Bain du Soleil," Grace pointed out, her voice sharp.

"Look, Grace." Roan's voice rose slowly. "You know I don't have any money."

"Not because you weren't offered an opportunity to make some," Grace said.

"Yeah, right," Roan snorted. "Cleaning up after everyone. Housemaid. That's a real job. And those were slave wages you wanted to pay. Forget it. I can get more money on the street."

"But notice that you aren't on the street right now, are you?" Grace said angrily. "You are sitting in a nice chair in back of a very nice house, using up *my* very nice suntan lotion. That no one gave you permission to use up."

"All right already," Roan said, sitting up and picking up the tubes. "Take the lotion. I don't care."

"Roan, that's not the point." Grace sighed and pulled over a chair. "Listen," she said. "Let's try again. I actually came home to talk to you about something."

"Okay," Roan said, reaching down to wipe a big glob of sun block from her toe and flicking it onto the sand.

"Roan," she said, "if you don't want to clean

the house because you feel like you're working for everyone else, why don't you work for yourself instead?" *And then,* Grace completed the thought silently, *you can waste your own expensive lotion.*

"Doing what," Roan said, "selling lemonade?"

Grace knew Roan was putting on a bit of an act. She could hear the interest in her voice.

"Nope. Selling relaxation," Grace answered, smiling. "You know I have some beach stands. Well, today I lost one of my attendants. I need someone who wants a job to take her place. And I thought of you."

Grace leaned back and squinted into the bright blue sky.

"How much would it pay?" Roan asked. "Not that I'm saying yes or anything."

"Well, I offered you six dollars an hour to clean the house. This job is six dollars an hour to sit in the sun. To chat with the tourists. To see and be seen." Grace smiled.

"That sounds easy," Roan mumbled.

"It's the same pay for everyone," Grace said, "just in case you think I'm trying to take advantage of you. It's a job, Roan. Out of the house. On the beach."

"Sounds cool."

"Maybe you'd better think about it some," Grace suggested, yawning and getting up out of the chair. "You might not be interested."

"What do you say that for now, after offering it to me?" Roan asked angrily.

"Well, it's a fun job. And it's pretty cushy, if you ask me. But there's one thing you'd have to remember." Grace's voice was stern. "It is still a job. And a job means every day, not just the days you feel like it. It's responsibility, Roan. Don't take the job unless you think you can handle the responsibility."

Roan didn't answer right away.

"I need someone right away," Grace said after a few minutes of silence. "If you don't want it, I'll go find someone else."

"No," Roan said quickly. "I mean, you don't need to do that, I guess." She was stumbling over her words, and she blushed. "I can do you this favor, Grace," she said calmly. "Sure. If you need someone, I can help you out."

"I don't want your help, Roan," Grace said. "I want to know if you want this job. For the whole summer."

"That's what I said, isn't it?" Roan snapped. "The whole summer. Fine, I'll take it. When do I start?"

"Tomorrow morning," Grace said, grinning broadly. "You'll come with me, and I'll show you what you have to do, okay?"

"Okay," Roan said.

Grace turned to go back into the house, but at the sliding door she stopped and looked back at Roan. "Thanks," she said. "I'm glad I could count on you."

"Now, I know this looks scary," Marta said to the little boy in front of her, "but it's really not so bad." It had been a long day and this was her last patient. Just one more blood test to get through. She was holding a small blue plastic cylinder that looked like a corkscrew.

"What's that for?" the little dark-haired boy said.

"It's to test your blood," she said. "We want to find out why you don't feel so good." Marta took the boy's hand and held it tightly. She placed the plastic tube against his finger.

"What if it hurts?" the boy asked.

"If it really hurts, I'll give you a ride in my chair afterward," Marta said. "Is that a fair trade?"

The little boy looked down at the shiny metal and big wheels of her chair. "How fast can you go?" he asked.

"Oh, I don't know," Marta said, "maybe about—seventy miles an hour!"

She was watching him carefully. Just as he spoke, she poked him with her needle.

"Wow—ow!" he said, his eyes wide and surprised.

"All done," she said, smiling. "Now, did that hurt?"

The boy looked confused. "I don't know," he said. "I mean, I think so, but it was too fast."

"I can always do it again, if you're not sure," Marta said.

"Oh no, it's okay," the little boy said quickly, smiling at her like an angel. "I'm sure it didn't hurt. I think. But can I still get a ride?"

They came down the hall speeding, almost running over Jill, the new part-time nurse's aide.

"I took this job because this is a clinic," she called after them. "I thought I would be *safe* here!"

The little boy was on Marta's lap as they came screeching around the corner into the waiting room. Marta rolled to a stop in front of the boy's mother.

"Mom!" the boy said, his eyes shining. "That was great! Can we get one too?"

His mother frowned and shook her head, giving Marta an apologetic look. "I'm sorry, honey, we really can't."

"They're not always as much fun as that," Marta said.

"You can come to my house to play anytime you want," the little boy said, waving to her as his mother led him from the clinic.

Marta waved good-bye and checked her

watch. Another long day over, she thought. She turned her chair and jumped in her seat when she found herself staring into a pair of coal-black eyes. Dominic was sitting on a bench across the waiting room, watching her with a mixture of pity and something else. Regret? But the look was fleeting, and disappeared as he smiled warmly and stood to come over to her.

"Are you finished for the night?" he asked softly.

"Why?" Marta found herself asking. "Do I have other plans?"

Dominic looked blank for a moment. Then he said quietly, "I thought we might go out and get something to eat."

"Obviously that's what you thought," Marta said. "Does this mean you're now asking what *I* think?"

"Yes," Dominic said slowly, his eyes darkening. "Okay, that's what I'm doing. Asking. Would you like to get something to eat with me?"

Marta thought for a minute, willing herself to keep quiet. What was the matter with her? She had been in a fine mood today. But the moment she saw Dominic, she felt agitated and her whole body had gone tight. She wasn't even thinking about what she was saying, and she definitely wasn't saying anything nice. She took a deep breath and looked him in the eye.

"Sure," she said. "Let's get some dinner."

They went for pizza, which was becoming their habit. It was the only thing they could ever agree on. At the restaurant, Dominic ordered a large pepperoni and black olive, the same pie they'd had last time.

"You seem to be pretty sure of yourself," Marta snapped. "Aren't you even going to ask me what I want?"

Dominic blushed with embarrassment.

"I'm sorry," he said. "What would you like to get?"

"I don't know," Marta said angrily. "Maybe that's fine. But the point is, you didn't even ask. What if I *had* wanted something different. There's not a lot I can change about my life." Her voice started to rise. "At least small pleasures can add some excitement. Or don't you think my feelings matter?"

Dominic turned to look at her, his black eyes shining. For a moment, just a second really, Marta was afraid of him. But then it passed as he took a breath, and his eyes didn't look stormy, just very, very sad.

"Of course your feelings matter," he said softly. "Why don't you tell me what you want, so we can order. There are other people waiting."

Suddenly Marta felt completely ashamed. Then she looked at Dominic, and her own eyes started blazing with anger. It was his fault that she had embarrassed herself like this. His fault that he hadn't asked what she wanted, that he'd made her yell. Her mind balked at her next thought, but it came unbidden; his fault that she was in this chair.

"We don't want to keep them waiting for a cripple," she hissed, turning her wheelchair from the counter. "Excuse me," she snapped at a young couple. "I'm not feeling hungry anymore." They parted and let her pass. Dominic was right behind her.

Outside, he caught up with her in the crowd and grabbed her arm.

"What's wrong with you," Dominic demanded. "What did I do?"

Marta's eyes went wide with false shock. "What did you do?" she screeched. "How quickly we forget," she sneered. "Don't you remember anymore? You just told me two days ago. You shot me!"

Dominic winced and closed his eyes. He was breathing heavily.

"Marta," he moaned, his hands on her arms.

"I seem to be sleeping terribly lately," she went on. "Last night I dreamed about being back in the hospital. You know what they call it, I'm sure. Rehab."

Dominic was looking straight at her now. His eyes were shining, wet with tears.

"Rehabilitation," Marta went on, her heart hardening with every word. "Teaching me how to live again. As if *I* had lost that ability. As if it were my fault. Being in the wrong place at the wrong time."

"I'm so sorry, Marta," Dominic said. "I'm so sorry. Of course it was never your fault. It was mine."

"Oh stop already!" Marta yelled. "Stop being there, stop saying you're sorry. Stop trying to take the blame. It's too late! I already took the bullet!"

A small crowd of beachgoers had gathered around them. The lights of the boardwalk were coloring them bright yellow, pink, and purple. But Marta and Dominic hardly noticed.

Dominic was on his knees now in front of her. "I was wrong," he whispered. "What can I do?" he said quietly. "I'll do anything I can to help."

Marta gripped the wheels of her chair and spun them. Her chair shot backward away from him.

"No!" she shouted. "It's too late. *I* was the one who was wrong. I don't want your help. Or your pity, dammit." Marta's voice was shaking. "I don't want to see you again. Ever. I thought I could forgive and forget. Or at least forget." She smacked her hands down on the armrests of her chair. "But I can never forget. Every minute of every day, I remember. I'm stuck in this chair forever. I'll always remember!"

Roan jumped on Bo's skateboard, and he took her hand, towing her through the crowd on the boardwalk.

"So what do you want to do?" Roan asked suggestively.

"Do you want to play a game?" Bo asked, pointing at one of the arcades.

"Like what?"

"I dunno," he said. "Shoot the basketball. Knock down the milk cans. Toss the little rings?"

"What for?"

"I dunno," Bo said. "Because it's fun."

"Is it?"

"Come on." Bo grabbed her hand and took her to one of the stalls people were gathered around. It was the calendar game. There were colored squares with every month of the year painted all around the stall. Bo took out fifty cents.

"Step up, step up," the man in the stall was yelling. "Hurry, hurry, place your bets, pick your month, pick your color, best odds on the board-walk!"

Bo turned to Roan. "When's your birthday?" he asked her.

"August," Roan said. "But I doubt that's a lucky month."

Bo put his money on the purple square marked August. "This is a pretty lucky game," Bo told her. "If he picks purple, we get a small prize, and if he picks August, we get an even bigger one."

The man in the stall shook a bucket of small wooden squares. Then he reached a hand in and pulled one out.

"Here's a winner," he yelled, "here's a winner. Step up, step up! Play to win. We've got a winner! The little lady with the blond hair, and what would you like, my dear?"

Roan chose a small stuffed animal, purple for her winning color. A small purple horse with a yellow mane. When the man in the stall gave it to her, she squealed and clapped her hands. Then she leaned over and gave Bo a quick kiss on the cheek.

"Let's stop now while we're ahead," she said. "One game, one win. That's a great record."

"Okay," Bo said. "Do you want to just walk?"

"I want to ride," Roan said, laughing.

Bo gave her his skateboard again and took her hand, towing her beside him.

"Sometimes I think this place is really cool," Roan said, looking at all the food stalls and the couples giggling and laughing with each other.

"It's all right, I guess," Bo said. "It's different if you live here all the time."

"Have you always lived here?" Roan asked.

"Yeah, but not where we are now. I used to live in this big apartment building on the top floor. My mom liked it better than a house."

"What does your mom do, anyway? She must be away a lot," Roan said. "I've been wondering why Grace acts so in charge all the time."

Bo pulled her through the crowd to the edge of the boardwalk where they could look at the ocean.

"My mom *is* away a lot," Bo said. "And Grace *is* in charge all the time. My mom's dead."

"Oh, sorry." Roan put her hand to her mouth and started chewing on her thumbnail. "That's harsh, huh?"

"Yeah," Bo said. "I loved her and all, but she wasn't the greatest mom. She drank a lot. All the time, actually. That's how she died. She went swimming in the ocean. But she was too drunk and she drowned."

"Wow," Roan said, looking out at the water. "Out there?"

Bo nodded.

"Is that why Grace doesn't drink?"

"I guess so," Bo said slowly. "She doesn't want to end up dead too."

They were both quiet for a long time. Roan felt Bo's hand in hers, warm and soft and sweaty. He looked away from her and gave her hand a little squeeze. She tightened her grip, and she could see him blush.

"Yeah," Roan said softly. "Well, since you told me about your mom, I'll tell you about mine. She doesn't drink so much, but I would if I were her. She's got a terrible life. She's got this boyfriend. He's a real bastard."

"Why," Bo asked. "What does he do? Does he hit her?"

"Yeah," Roan whispered. "He hits her a lot. And then sometimes he does worse."

Bo winced. "Wow. Your poor mom. Did she ever call the police?"

Roan nodded. "She tried to. But he always stopped her. He always knew what she was doing, and then he would punish her even worse. He hurt her a lot."

"And she didn't do anything? Why didn't she leave?"

Roan turned and looked at Bo. She leaned close to him and put her lips to his ear.

"It wasn't her," Roan whispered. "It was me. And I did leave."

Roan felt Bo's hands on her arms. He was holding her tightly. Not pulling her toward him, or pushing her away. Just holding her there.

"I'm sorry," he said, his voice full of sympathy.

Suddenly Roan pulled back and laughed.

"Yeah," she said lightly, "so am I. That's why I

need a little something, you know? To take my mind off it. To get rid of bad memories." Roan cocked her head and looked at him. "Do you have bad memories, Bo?"

He nodded slowly.

"So let's stop the sob stories," Roan whispered, "and go get a little something to make us feel better."

ELEVEN

"Haven't we been through this scene recently?" Kate asked as she watched Chelsea outline her lips with a vibrant red liner. They were both in the upstairs bathroom with makeup bags, brushes, hair spray, and gel scattered on the counter before them.

Chelsea laughed. Last time they were getting ready to go out for the evening, Chelsea, Kate, Marta, and Grace had ended up in the laundry room singing corny old songs.

"Well, no breaking out in show tunes this time, okay?" Chelsea said. "At least no songs from a story where the hero dies in the end."

"How about if he comes back to life?" Kate asked quietly.

Chelsea's hand stopped, the liner pencil resting in the middle of her lower lip. Was she hear-

111

ing correctly? That was definitely a wistful note in Kate's voice. Kate had claimed to be taking Justin's reappearance in stride. Now it seemed Kate still had a few questions.

Chelsea loved Justin as a good friend, and as a boyfriend for her best friend. She had always understood what the differences between Justin and Kate were; she had never understood how Kate let those differences get in the way of love. Love was love, wasn't it? You took it where you found it. You didn't worry about differences, or consequences, or reality, did you?

That had certainly been the old Chelsea, wanting to take love where she found it. Never worrying about differences or consequences. Or reality. And now she was a married woman about to go out on a date with someone other than her husband. She had ignored all of the potential problems between herself and Connor. In spite of what everyone, Kate most of all, had told her. She had ignored them for love. And look where she was now.

"I don't know," Chelsea finally answered softly. "The answer depends on whether we're talking about a love story complete with orchestra and dance numbers on a Broadway stage, or real life going on day to day in a beach resort."

Kate nodded and sighed. "Maybe I'm wondering if real life can ever be a love story complete with orchestra," she said.

Suddenly the floor below them started to shake. The stereo blasting in the living room.

Kate and Chelsea looked at each other in the mirror and then broke out laughing.

"Well, it's not an orchestra," Chelsea said.

"How do you do that, anyway?" Kate asked, watching Chelsea put liner around her eyes with a steady hand while the rest of her body shimmied to the music.

Chelsea winked. "Secrets of an artist," she said slyly, and stepped back to admire herself. She was wearing a bright yellow sleeveless top with crossing straps in the back, a pair of vibrant royal-blue cropped pants, and black sandals.

"Will I knock him dead?" Chelsea asked.

Kate smiled and nodded. "He's going to knock himself dead for ever letting you cross the road," she said.

Chelsea's smile faltered. "Oh, Kate. I'm sorry—I didn't tell you, did I? I'm not going out with Connor."

Kate's brow creased in confusion, and her face turned red.

"Oh, no, I'm sorry. I assumed, after last time—"

"You mean because my last date was such a disaster I would go right back to Connor?" Chelsea finished for her.

"Not exactly," Kate said lamely.

"It's all right, Kate," Chelsea said, smiling. "I know what you mean. I guess I probably thought that would happen too. And I didn't plan on meeting Paul Hagen today either. But I did. And so here I am."

"So who is he?" Kate asked. "Where did you meet him?"

"On the boardwalk. He saw me sketching and he thought my work was great," Chelsea said excitedly. "He really thinks I have a lot of talent, not like some other people who shall remain nameless but who don't appreciate what I'm trying to do with my life."

"Oh, Chelsea, that's not really fair," Kate said. "Of course Connor appreciates you. And I know he thinks you are incredibly talented. He's just having trouble with his own direction, and maybe seeing you so sure of yourself is hard for him."

"Well, anyway, that's not the point now," Chelsea said, shaking her head. "The point is that Paul runs a branch office for a big New York advertising agency, and—" Chelsea paused. Kate leaned forward, waiting. "He wants to hire me!" Chelsea screeched.

Kate screamed too, and they grabbed each other and whirled around the bathroom.

"*And* Paul is a wonderfully handsome and

charming man," Chelsea continued. "And a bit older."

"Older is good," Kate agreed.

"He's like B.D.," Chelsea said. "If B.D. wasn't my brother."

"Not being siblings is a definite plus. And you look great," Kate said, giving Chelsea a squeeze on the arms. "Have a wonderful time."

"This is really creepy, Roan," Bo said as he dropped down beside her on the sand. They were far up the beach, and Roan was taking him under the boardwalk. It smelled like dead fish and garbage, and another familiar scent to Bo. The smell of alcohol. The smell of drunks. And there was another smell, a sweet smoky smell that he didn't recognize.

"Look, Bo," she said, turning on him, her eyes angry for a moment before she smiled and laughed. "Don't be a scaredy-cat. You're old enough to take care of yourself, aren't you?" she asked sweetly. She reached out and took his hand. "Besides," she said, "I want you to stay with me."

Bo didn't really want to go on, and it wasn't because she had called him afraid. Something wasn't right. He felt it. But he couldn't let Roan walk away without him. He didn't want to leave her. He thought of turning away, and his stomach tightened in knots as he looked at her white-gold hair shimmering in the darkness, and her large eyes asking him to stay.

"Come on," she said, pulling his hand. "We'll have fun. I promise."

She turned, and Bo followed her until they heard the low laughter of other people sitting in the shadows.

"Hey, Billy," Roan called out. "Come here and meet my friend Bo."

A blond-haired boy, shirtless and in rolled-up black jeans, stepped from the shadows. His chest was pale and scrawny.

Billy took in Bo with one glance. "Does your mama know where you are, punk?"

"Shut up, Billy," Roan snapped. "He's cool."

Roan turned to Bo. "Listen," she said, "I'll be back in a minute."

She took Billy by the arm and they stepped away into the shadows. Bo could hear them talking, and he could hear Roan's low laugh. He heard the sound of a match and saw the fire lift to the end of a cigarette. He could see Roan bending toward the flame, inhaling.

Roan and Billy came back to him, and he saw that it wasn't a cigarette she was holding. There was the smell he hadn't recognized before.

Roan held the joint out to him. "Here, Bo," she said.

Bo leaned back against one of the wooden pilings and shook his head. "No, thanks," he said.

"He's a geek," Billy said to Roan, taking the joint from her. "Why'd you bring him, anyway?"

"'Cause I like him," she said. "Leave him alone, all right?"

When they'd finished the joint, Roan came over to Bo and leaned against him. She was giggling, and she reached up and put her fingers in his hair.

"Hey, Bo," she said in his ear. "I can still make you feel high, you know."

Bo closed his eyes. He liked the way it felt, her leaning against him, her closeness. But there was something he didn't want. Something that made him sick inside at the same time as he thought of putting his arms around her. He didn't want her like this. He didn't know who this girl was.

He opened his eyes and shook her off and stepped back.

"I feel fine, now," he said.

Billy moved over to them and reached into his pocket.

"What's the matter with you, man?" Billy asked menacingly. "You got a problem with her?"

"No problem," Bo said. "I don't have the problem."

"You saying I've got a problem?" Billy's hand

came out of his pocket, holding a knife. Bo backed away a bit, his eyes locked on the knife.

"Wait, Bo," Roan said, stumbling in front of Billy. "Thanks for the weed, Billy, but I gotta split. Glad I can always count on you to make me feel fine. See ya."

Bo scrambled out from under the boardwalk and walked north on the beach. Toward home. Roan caught up to him and took his arm and held it against her.

"Bo," she whined. "What's wrong. Don't you like me anymore? I like you, you know. We could have a real good time together."

Bo kept his head down as they walked.

"I like you," he answered. "I like you a lot."

He thought of all the times he had seen his sister the way Roan was now. He knew why they had called her Racey Gracie in high school. Racey Gracie. Fast and loose. He'd even gotten into a few fights about it.

But Grace was different now. He saw it, and he knew that everyone else saw it too. Justin, Chelsea, Marta. Even Kate. They didn't just like Grace. They respected her now.

"I just don't like you stoned," he said to Roan, his eyes straight ahead. Roan let go of his arm. But he reached out and took her hand. They walked along together in silence, holding hands, looking at the stars.

*   *   *

"So have I told you how beautiful you look tonight?" Paul asked.

"Well," Chelsea said, scolding him, "only about six or seven times."

"You don't remember?" Paul said, feigning hurt.

"You know us artists," Chelsea said, sighing. "No head for numbers, just bodies."

"I'll drink to that," Paul said, looking at her appreciatively.

They were at The Hurricane Lamp, a fancy restaurant on the bay. They had a nice view of the water, and their table was lit with the soft light from a flickering hurricane lamp.

Very romantic, Chelsea thought. Good service. Quiet, older clientele. And the lamps. Paul's smile was glowing at her from the darkness.

"Well, don't drink too much of that club soda," Chelsea said jokingly. "We don't want those little bubbles going to your head. You're too big for me to carry you out of here."

Paul laughed loudly, a friendly, comforting sound.

"At least now I know you'd try. You have a great sense of humor, Chelsea."

Chelsea smiled, and her cheeks turned red. She did have a great sense of humor. Only, no one had told her that for a long time. Connor was the comedian in their relationship. That was one

119

of the things that had really irritated her. He made everything into a joke. It wasn't a sense of humor with him, it was a way of life.

"Which leads me to the next topic of conversation," Paul said. "You need to have a sense of humor to work for me. In advertising, we take the clients we're given. And if the product isn't something we would like or use, we need to find a way to convince ourselves otherwise. Because if we can convince ourselves, then we can convince anyone. It's fun," Paul said. "But it's serious work."

"I can handle serious work," Chelsea replied quickly, "even if some people think I'm not ready."

Paul looked at her quizzically.

"It's nothing," Chelsea said, waving her hand.

Paul gazed at her a moment as if he were looking for something, as if he had some suspicion about her. Then he glanced down at her hands and smiled.

"Well, I'm not one of those people," Paul said.

While they ate clams casino and poached salmon, Paul outlined a few of the projects he was working on: a new suntan lotion, a beach store specializing in windsurfing gear, a small boardwalk crab joint, and even a campaign for the Ocean City Grand Hotel.

"I'd better not work for that one," Chelsea

said, laughing. "I have to admit I don't have the best history with them."

"Why?" Paul asked. "What happened?"

"To make a long story short, there was a contest, 'Best Body on the Beach,' and a few people ended up going to jail—"

"Did you win?" Paul interrupted.

"Well, no—" Chelsea said, blushing.

"Then whoever went to jail deserved it," Paul said. "Any more to that story?"

Chelsea laughed. "I guess not. I'll work on whatever you ask me to."

"Why don't you give me a couple of drawings for the suntan lotion? Can you have some ready by Monday?" Paul asked.

Chelsea nodded.

"Okay, then," he continued. "I'll take a look at what you've done, and we'll move on from there. At least with respect to your career. For now," Paul said, "if you're done, we can move on from here, and you can let me walk you home."

They walked easily together, chatting happily about Ocean City, the weather—whatever. There was something so easy about being with Paul, Chelsea thought, thinking again of her brother. She was relaxed and completely unself-conscious with him. They stopped when they neared the house.

"It's pretty nice, isn't it?" Chelsea asked.

Paul gave a low whistle. "Maybe you should be offering me some work," he said jokingly.

"It's not my place," Chelsea explained. "It belongs to a friend of mine, Grace. It even has a name," she said, laughing. "Landfall. Although I still don't think it's a name that inspires great comfort. I think I'll wake some night to find the ground opening and swallowing us up. But it's nice of Grace to let me stay with her, considering the circumstances—" Chelsea stopped short.

"What circumstances?" Paul asked softly, taking her hand.

"Oh, you know," Chelsea faltered, "starving artist and all. Can never be sure of the rent—"

Chelsea stopped speaking as Paul leaned down to kiss her. For a wild moment she almost pulled away. What if Connor saw? she thought. What if he was standing in the window right now, looking down on them? She was about to kiss another man. It wasn't right, not when you were married. Then the image of Connor on the boardwalk with his arms around the dark-haired girl came to her. Connor's face saying, "Maybe we should see other people."

As Paul's lips touched hers, her last thought was that she hoped Connor *was* standing there. She hoped he did see. She wasn't going to let him get the best of her.

The kiss was nice. But nothing more. Chelsea

felt it, and she knew Paul felt it too. He raised his head, but he didn't let go of her.

"What other circumstances, Chelsea?" he asked. "I'd like you to know you can tell me the truth."

Chelsea sighed, and her eyes filled with tears, but she blinked them away.

"I lived there," she said, her head nodding at the old Victorian behind them. "With my husband."

Paul nodded, and smiled.

"You're not surprised?" Chelsea asked.

"Well," he answered. "I had a feeling it was something like that. A fiancé anyway, if not quite marriage."

"How did you know?" Chelsea asked.

"Your artist's hands give you away, Chelsea. Your fingers don't seem to remember it, and they keep going to twist the ring that isn't there. I'm sure you don't even notice what you're doing. It hasn't been very long since you took it off, has it?"

Chelsea shook her head. "No," she whispered. "Not very long. I'm sorry."

"Don't be sorry, Chelsea. Even if you weren't married, I get the feeling that I wouldn't be the one for you. I find you incredibly attractive, and very sexy, and I'm bold enough to say I know you like me, but perhaps not in equal measure. It's okay," Paul said kindly. "It happens to the best of us."

123

Chelsea nodded, unsure of what to say.

"Well, thanks for dinner," she began, "and it was nice meeting you—"

"Wait a minute, Chelsea," Paul interrupted. "You sound like you're giving me the Big Goodbye. Don't forget I'm going to see you on Monday, aren't I? You said you'd have some artwork for me by then, or are you changing your mind about the work?"

Chelsea looked up quickly. "Oh no!" she said. "I'm not changing my mind—"

"But you thought I might be?" Paul asked. "I hope you know I'm not the kind of businessman who will lose a good artist because my kisses don't make her swoon."

"I'm sorry, Paul," Chelsea said.

"Don't be sorry," Paul said, laughing and giving her a hug. "Just be glad you met me—and have something great to show me on Monday."

"I am very glad I met you," Chelsea said, her smile genuine and happy. "And I will have something better than great to show you."

TWELVE

"Ahh, for shame, another miss." Connor sighed as the crumpled paper bounced off the rim of the black plastic garbage can across the room. So far his shooting percentage was well below fifty. He'd made about ten baskets, but forty points' worth of paper lay scattered around the room. He turned his chair back to his messy desk in the staff room of the local paper where he worked.

"Remember, Riordan," he told himself, "when you publish your books and become famous, you will look back at this time in your life and talk about it fondly."

He leaned back and his chair squeaked loudly.

"Yes, you see, my dear," he said, talking to his imaginary interviewer, "I got my start in the papers of course, as many have. Sacrificing my talents for the mainstream."

So many poets are reduced to this, aren't they? the interviewer would ask sympathetically.

"How true, how true," Connor replied. "Great artists are seldom recognized in their own lifetimes."

He sighed. *Enough of this daydreaming,* he said to himself. *Time to get something done.* He looked down at the blank paper before him and sneered. "Something witty and catchy, my boy, that's all you need," he said aloud. "Don't rack your brains too much. You'll get a headache, and then where will you be?"

It was late. He'd been here all night, trying his hand at copy for Denise. She worked in the advertising department and was running late on a deadline. She'd asked him earlier, most likely because he was the only grunt around, to see if he could help her come up with anything for the well-stocked Kmart clone in town.

He leaned over and scrawled a few lines into his notepad.

"This will have to do," he said, rising from his chair and ripping the top page away. He walked down the hall to one of the offices, knocked, entered, and handed Denise his masterpiece.

"Connor, this is great stuff," Denise said after

126

reading it through quickly. "You've got a fantastic sense of humor. Quite a gift. Blarney. Isn't that what they call it in Ireland?"

Connor smiled and ran a hand through his red hair, already standing on end from hours of similar treatment.

"That's what they call it," he said. *Although some people don't agree that it's a gift,* he finished silently.

"Let me show this to Chuck," she said. "I think he'll really appreciate it." She picked up a phone sitting on her desk and buzzed another office.

A few minutes later Chuck, the rumpled manager of advertising, came into her office.

"Here," Denise said, handing him the typed sheet of paper. "Read this. You'll enjoy it."

Chuck held the paper up and read aloud:

> "For special new, improved floor wax,
> a basketball, a brand-new fax,
> and panty hose that never run,
> or juicy hot dogs in your bun,
> we're certain that you won't find more
> anywhere than in our store."

There was a moment of silence, during which Connor was sure that Denise had vastly overestimated her boss's sense of humor. Then Chuck broke out in laughter.

"I love it!" he said. "It's wonderful. Perfect. Especially for this town."

"Well," Connor said, "it isn't Joyce."

"Joyce-shmoyce," Denise quipped, rolling her eyes. "This is advertising, not literature."

You mean great *literature*, Connor said to himself.

"Listen," Chuck said, "I know you're on the local beat right now—"

The deadbeat, you mean, Connor added.

"But we'll pass your name around if you're interested in doing any more work like this on the side," Chuck offered.

"Great," Connor said, a plastic smile on his face.

"And who knows." Denise grinned. "This may be where your true talents lie."

Connor nodded and shook their hands. *Lord, I hope not,* he thought as he left the office.

"How can you bear to eat here every day?" Tosh laughed as he and Kate pushed though the crowd outside of Floaters, the little restaurant at the south end of the boardwalk that was the lifeguard staff's almost official hangout.

Kate laughed and waved to one of her fellow guards. She stepped away from Tosh for a moment, to chat with her coworker. Kate watched as Tosh continued into the crowd. She could see his head above most everyone else's. Kate took a

128

few steps toward him before she saw the dark-haired girl at his side. She was wearing the shortest denim shorts that Kate had ever seen, and a tiny black bikini top. Tosh's arm was around her, resting on her waist, and he bent down to speak in her ear. Kate saw the girl giggle and lean into him, rubbing herself against his side.

Then Tosh looked over his shoulder and saw Kate.

His face didn't change expression at all, although his hand dropped from the girl's waist as he smiled.

"Hey, Kate," Tosh said as she reached them. He easily slid an arm around her shoulder and pulled her against him. "This is Jennie. She's from New York."

Kate smiled. "Nice to meet you," she said, extending her hand. Jennie didn't take it, and Kate let it drop back to her side.

"So this is Kate," Jennie said slyly, looking her up and down.

"Has he told you about me?" Kate asked.

"Sure," Jennie said, "when he gets a chance to breathe—"

Tosh laughed and interrupted her. "Always a kidder, Jennie," he said, smiling at her. Tosh turned to Kate. "Jennie belongs to the same health club back in the New York. Quite a surprise running into her here, wouldn't you say?"

He smiled sweetly. "She was probably about to tell you what a failure I am in the weight room. And you know me, Kate. I just can't bear to be made fun of." He rolled his eyes in mock humor.

"You lift weights?" Kate looked at Jennie incredulously.

"Don't let her size fool you," Tosh said before Jennie could answer. "She's an animal."

Jennie smiled. "And don't you forget it," she said to Tosh, and turned away. "Nice to meet you," she called out over her shoulder.

Kate and Tosh moved in and found an empty table. They managed to sit and order from a passing waitress at the same time.

"So, what a surprise," Kate began.

Tosh put down his water glass and stared her straight in the eye. "You want to ask me about Jennie," he said. "Go ahead and ask. You want to know who she is and how I know her? I told you. I know her from the City. She's from my past, Kate. We all have a past, remember? But unlike some people, I'm able to keep my past where it belongs and get on with my present." He reached across the table and took her hand. "And my future," he said. "Honestly," he continued in a hurt voice, "of the two of us, I can't believe my past is the one we need to worry about."

Kate looked away and blushed. He was right. Kate had sensed something strange from Jennie, as though Jennie knew something personal about her that no one else should know. Kate had felt a glimmer of competitiveness, and she had started to feel suspicious. But here Tosh was again, anticipating her feelings. He knew what Kate was thinking about him before she'd said a word, and he had put everything on the table and told her what she wanted to know.

Kate blushed, and guilt flared through her stomach, making her feel queasy. Just last night she had sat on the beach kissing Justin, letting him kiss her, hold her, touch her. She had been on the verge of doing a lot more than running into an old friend in a crowded restaurant.

"At least my past doesn't come back from the dead," Tosh said, watching her carefully. "You know we haven't talked about this at all. And I don't want to push you, because I know it's probably difficult for you."

How can anyone be so understanding? Kate thought.

"But I have to say how I feel," Tosh went on. "Justin had quite a few weeks to let someone know he was alive. But he didn't want to do that. Better," he continued, "to let the people who cared about him go on thinking that he'd died, and wander back to Ocean City in his own time. Just roll into town and show up at your house as if nothing had happened." Tosh leaned back in his chair and looked at her narrowly. "Not particularly responsible, I'd say. But certainly more interesting, right Kate?"

She didn't answer him. She couldn't.

"Much more interesting," Tosh continued, seeing her confusion, "and easier, of course, not to think about other people. Not to worry that other people's emotions were at stake. But then again, he must have depended on the fact that when he sauntered into your house one day, you'd be so happy to see him there, he wouldn't have to explain anything. Not his silence after he was found." Tosh paused. "What a charmer. I can see exactly why it was so difficult for you to let go." He sneered. "I can see that he really cared a lot for you. He really considered you an individual, with a life that might actually go on without him."

Somehow Kate knew that what Tosh was saying was unfair. But then again, it was all true. Why was she sitting here feeling like she ought to defend Justin, when she herself had accused him of all the same things? A lack of respect for her own goals and desires. An unwillingness to see that he had always wanted her to sacrifice for their relationship without being willing to do the same himself. An irresponsibility with his life. An aimlessness. An interest only in the life he wanted to live. A life without goals, she'd thought. Unchallenging.

Justin had never wanted to be challenged.

Not by her, not by anyone. Not by anything. Perhaps the idea of calling her right away had been a challenge. Or a burden, Kate thought. Or perhaps it was true that Justin didn't really care how she might have felt thinking that he'd drowned.

All she knew was that it was hard to get a handle on her feelings. Tosh was telling the truth. And she was lying to him. Every moment that she didn't tell him about her meeting with Justin on the beach.

Finally their food came. For the first time in a long time, they ate in silence. But Kate looked at him, and she could see that Tosh wasn't angry at her. He was giving her time to think. Time to think about what he'd said. Time to think for herself what she wanted. What she was going to do now that Justin had returned? And again, like always, Tosh wasn't going to push her. He would wait for her decision.

When they finished eating, Tosh went to pay the check, and Kate gave up their table to a desperate-looking couple and went to stand by the door. It seemed to be taking Tosh a long time, and Kate started searching the room for him, but she didn't see him anywhere. She pushed her way outside, but Tosh wasn't there. As soon as she got back inside, someone in the crowd grabbed at her from behind and she yelped.

"Hey, it's me," Tosh said in her ear. "You all right?"

"Yeah, I'm all right," Kate said, shaking her head. "You startled me," she explained. "I wasn't sure who it was, and I thought for a moment I'd lost you."

Tosh put his arm around her and steered her through the door, but not before Kate heard a voice giggling and whispering loudly behind her. "You already have," it said. Kate was sure the voice was Jennie's.

When Connor finally arrived home, he found Justin standing on the small balcony of the apartment, staring at the house across the street.

"Hey you—Peeping Tom! And a lifeguard at that. You must take your job seriously to be doing it at night. Any lights on over there, by the way?" Connor asked casually.

Justin flinched and stepped back into the apartment.

"Sorry, didn't hear you come in," Justin said. He fell onto the couch and sank toward its sagging center. "Actually, no." He forced a chuckle. "Dark as the ocean over there. I guess everyone is out tonight."

"Everyone?" Connor asked.

Justin looked up at him and was about to speak. But their eyes locked, and both of their interests in the house across the street were plain as day. *We may talk to each other like we don't care,* Connor thought, *but we do. We both do. For two people in particular.*

Justin nodded sympathetically. "Everyone," he said.

"Just as well," Connor quipped, turning away. "More people on the boardwalk means more business in town, and more business in town means more news and more advertising, which means more work for me in my new chosen career."

"And that's how you're going to think about it?" Justin asked. "Sounds like a lot of work to be that generous."

"It's not generosity," Connor replied. "It's the only way to get through the day."

"There's an airmail letter for you, by the way," Justin said, pointing to the small table by the front door. "I hope it's better news than last time."

Last time, Connor thought. When Molly, his old girlfriend from Ireland, showed up to tell him that he was the proud father of a baby girl. Well, that hadn't been true, but it had been pretty harrowing just the same. He and Chelsea had been stuck with the baby for a week before they'd been able to go to New York to give it back to Molly.

"I can't imagine anything could be much worse than that," Connor said. He looked at the postmark before he opened it.

"It's from my mum and dad," he said. "I wonder what news they could have to tell." He tore it open and tried to pull out a small folded sheet of airmail paper.

"I hate this stuff," Connor complained, tearing a piece of his letter. "I'll be lucky if I can get this out in less than seventeen pieces. I hope light news is good news."

Justin put his feet up on the table in front of him and turned on the small TV set. He started flipping through the stations.

"Hmm," Connor said, quickly scanning the letter. "According to this, they'll be arriving here in about a week."

Connor went into the kitchenette and came back with a bottle of Guinness. He flopped down into a chair and took a long swallow.

"I notice that's one of the only items you're able to keep stocked." Justin laughed.

"Et tu, Brute?" Connor asked, looking at Justin.

Justin's face scrunched up in confusion. "What did you just say?"

"Never mind. Literary allusion," Connor replied. "It's what you say when you're betrayed by one of your closest friends. You sound just like my wife, is all."

"Oh," Justin said, wincing. "Sorry."

"Yes, well, don't apologize. She was right and so are you. I do seem to have trouble thinking of other needs. Like food."

Connor clenched the letter in his hand.

"So your parents are coming to America?" Justin asked. "Have they ever been here?"

"Nope," Connor said. "Oh, there," he yelped, pointing at the TV. "Stop."

Justin paused his finger on the remote.

"My parents believe America is the decadent West of great TV shows like this one," Connor explained, nodding at the gaudily dressed women prancing across the screen.

"And you haven't bothered to explain to them that it's not exactly the way it is on TV?" Justin asked.

"Well," Connor said, "look outside. Whatever I tried to tell them would probably seem a lie as soon as they got a look at this place at night."

Justin laughed. "I see your predicament. Ocean City may not be the best example of wholesome American living."

"No, and now isn't the best time for an example of devoted Irish parenting," Connor remarked.

"Why not?" Justin asked. "Don't you want to see your parents?"

"Sure I want to see them." Connor's smile was crooked. "But they're coming here to meet

Chelsea. And besides a thorough dissertation on the reality of the general American experience, there's one or two points about her that I haven't yet brought up in my letters."

Justin nodded slowly and smiled. "And exactly what points are those?" he asked.

"Oh," Connor said lightly, "a few minor details. Number one, that she isn't exactly Irish."

Justin raised his eyebrows.

"Number two, that she certainly isn't white."

Justin's smile disappeared.

"And of course number three, which granted is a relatively new condition," Connor said, taking a deep breath and looking around the small apartment sadly, "that she doesn't seem to be living with me anymore."

THIRTEEN

Kate sat on a chair on the deck, holding a cup of warm tea between her hands. It was still dark and she was shivering a little. She had been outside for over an hour, waiting for the sun to rise. Waiting to see if she had figured anything out yet. Waiting to see what she would do today. Because after last night, she knew that she had to do something.

After they'd come home from dinner, Tosh had kept silent. He'd been with her, next to her on the couch as they watched the news, next to her in bed as they read for an hour, next to her after she'd turned out the light to sleep. But he hadn't said a word. It was his way of backing off. Not physically, though. He held her hand, and touched her. He wasn't rejecting her. But by saying nothing, he was telling her something very important.

139

He wanted her to make a decision. That was all he was asking for. A decision. Finally, after everything they'd been through, he was telling her that he was unsure. That he didn't know where he stood with her now that Justin was back.

That was the question Kate had been asking herself all night. It was what she was asking herself now, as she watched the sun begin to rise over the ocean before her. Had she stayed with Tosh because he'd been nearby, because he was the next-best thing when she'd thought Justin was dead? Or had she truly chosen him?

Kate had thought she'd already made that decision. But it was true that she hadn't. Not really. She had taken Tosh, who was alive, over Justin when Justin was dead. That was a choice anyone could make. Life or death. Move on with your future or spend your life dwelling on the past.

But now she really did have to choose. Tosh or Justin. And this time, they were both alive.

With an effort, Kate put them both out of her mind. Just for a moment. For the few moments it took for the sun to rise fully and shine down on her. A few moments to listen to the sound of the waves washing up onto shore. The sound of the gentle splashing seemed to echo the length of the deserted beach.

The ocean was a constant, Kate thought. Something you could always count on. It was so huge, it was hundreds of places at one time. Thousands of boats sailed on it, millions of fish swam in it. It was traversed daily by dinghies, investigated by divers, emptied by fisherman, ridden by water-skiers and windsurfers. But always, every day at the same time, the waves would wash against the shore onto this part of the beach in the same way. The tides could not be changed. They came from the deepest places of the ocean, governed by something much larger than a few animals or people.

That was why Kate admired the sea. Why she had always felt so comfortable in the water. And so strong. She wanted to be that constant. She wanted to have those depths. Her depths were her goals and dreams and ambitions. She wanted something greater from her life. It was the drive that would keep her steady as the tides, and carry her exactly where she wanted to go.

She sat there in the sun until she was warm, and then she got up and went around the house and across the street. It was time to find Justin.

The banging wouldn't stop. Connor had been dreaming all night in terrible rhyming couplets: traveling cases for cassettes, volleyballs and brand-new nets, suntan lotion SPF 10, a typewriter, a grill, a pen, running shoes for summer runs, diet cola, water guns . . .

It could just be my head pounding, Connor thought. But when he opened his eyes, the noise was still there. Someone was knocking on his door. He saw his alarm clock glowing at him in the darkened room. Six thirty in the morning! He was definitely being tortured.

"Oh, Joyce," he moaned. "James Joyce, your ghost is haunting me. I know it was terrible. Terrible, terrible writing. Beneath me, of course."

He dragged himself out of bed, stumbled from his room, and found the front door.

Not too many people in the world were this persistent. Parents? But they weren't arriving for another week. Chelsea? Dream on, he told himself. The police? He was legally married, of course, but seeing as how his wife had left him, it was possible that this was Immigration.

How had they found him? Colleen, the Irish illegal he had helped the other day? Perhaps she had led them here.

"Oh, where is loyalty anymore?" he moaned. Then he straightened up and opened the door.

"Hey, Connor," Kate said. "Uh, did I wake you?"

Connor cocked an eyebrow, although the eye below it stayed closed. "Why on earth do you ask?" he said. "Don't I look as though I've been up for hours?"

"Actually, no," Kate admitted. "You look like someone just dragged you out of bed at"—she checked her watch and blushed—"six thirty. Oops, sorry," she said. "I know it's early, but it's important." She was trying to peer into the apartment over his shoulder.

"Please, Kate," he said, moving back. "How rude of me. But my excuse is that I'm still asleep. Come in."

Kate stepped inside. "Is Justin here?"

They both looked at the couch. The covers were thrown back and it was empty.

"It doesn't look like it," Connor said. "You're welcome to come in and wait."

"Oh, thanks anyway, Connor." Kate smiled. "But I really need to talk to him. I'll try to find him myself, thanks."

"No problem," he said as he closed the door behind her. "Thanks for waking me. I was running out of material anyway."

Connor tried, but he couldn't get back to sleep. He got up and wandered around his room for a while, touching the books on his homemade shelves, the tiny portable typewriter he'd found in New York, the small stack of paper where he'd tried to put down some of his thoughts into acceptable words. But his room was too empty to contain him.

He dressed and went outside. He hadn't been up this early since his days working construction last summer. It felt good to see sunlight at seven in the morning. His eyes were drawn across the street.

Come on, snap out of it, he said to himself. *Try to remember all the things that drove you crazy. Your room may be empty now, but would you rather have it this way, or not be able to see the floor at all?*

Still, he couldn't seem to drag himself away from the house. Was she awake yet? he wondered. What was she doing with herself now? He couldn't believe he had no idea about her life, what she was going to do when she woke up today. How was it possible that someone could become a stranger so quickly?

Suddenly, as he stood staring at the front door of Grace's house, it opened. Again, there was that moment when he thought, *Chelsea?*

But no. It was Tosh.

"Hey," Tosh called to him, and jogged across the street. "What are you up to this early? Loitering?"

"A little birdie woke me. And I was compelled to see the dawn," Connor quipped.

"Well, have you seen Kate by any chance?" Tosh asked.

"Yeah, actually, she's the one who woke me. She was looking for Justin—" Connor paused.

Tosh seemed unconcerned. "I figured as much," he said. "She has to speak to him

144

sooner or later. Good girl, Kate," he added softly. "So I guess we're free for the day," Tosh said happily. "What say we hit the beach and do a little sightseeing."

"Sightseeing?" Connor asked uneasily.

"It's all right, man," Tosh said, hitting Connor lightly on the arm. "My father raised me well. Look, just don't touch."

Connor paused for a moment.

"Come on," Tosh said, his voice confidential and understanding. "Don't forget I saw you standing here. We'll hold out until noon, and then we'll get a nice cold beer and sit in the sun. It'll make you feel better. At least for a few hours."

Connor sighed and nodded.

Kate had a feeling she knew where to find Justin. She crossed Ocean City toward the bay and walked along it until she neared the old run-down house they'd all lived in last summer. She could see Justin out on the dock by the boathouse, where he'd lived. And built *Kate*, his boat. Well, he'd helped build Kate the person a little too, she had to admit. She had grown a lot with him.

Justin was standing at the end of the dock, throwing sticks into the water for Mooch, who had turned back into a shaggy smelly saltwater boat mutt as soon as Justin had returned. Kate laughed to herself. So much for Grace's grand plans for doggie reform. Then she sighed. So much for her own plans with Justin. As much as she might want to, she couldn't make him into somebody he wasn't.

And she couldn't pretend to be someone else either. *Remember,* she said to herself, *you're the woman who chose not to sail away with him the last time. It shouldn't be any harder now,* she thought.

He heard the sound of her shoes on the dock as she approached, but he didn't turn. She came up and stood beside him.

"Justin," she said softly.

"Kate," he replied. "I thought that might be you. I couldn't figure on anyone else. Did you see?" he said, turning to look at the house behind him. "No one has rented it this summer. I wonder why."

"You sound sentimental." Kate smiled. "I wouldn't have thought it of you."

"No, I guess you wouldn't have," Justin answered.

Kate wanted to reply, but she bit her tongue. Surely he knew why she had followed him here. If bitterness would help him, she wouldn't fight back.

"I never thought we'd stand here together again," she said.

"I'm sorry about that," Justin said.

"I wonder if you know how much it hurt me," Kate mused. "I wonder if you understand what my world looked like when I thought that you were gone for good."

Justin sighed. "I know you hurt for me, Kate."

She turned to him then. "I hope you do," she said.

"It's just that you don't seem to be hurting anymore," Justin explained. "I still am, though."

"Justin, don't you see." Her voice was low and urgent. "I'm not with Tosh only because I thought you were dead. Justin, we went through this a year ago. You *left* me. And I *let* you go. Things don't change just because we are reminded somehow of our mortality. I'll tell you what hurt when I thought you were gone. I couldn't believe that you would never stand here again and throw sticks to your dog. That you wouldn't sit in the chair on the beach and watch over people, that you wouldn't save another life. It was such a waste! That's what I thought. A waste and a tragedy that someone so vital and so good could suddenly be gone."

Kate was holding him, looking in his eyes.

"And I couldn't believe that I would never see you again. But that was a selfish hurt. Because I already knew that it wasn't going to work between us. I missed you like that because I could.

147

Because I could pretend then that it might have worked. That it would have worked. Because as long as you weren't around, I could make us into the most wonderful couple that ever existed. It was something I wanted to believe. A fantasy I had. But it wasn't the truth."

"It was," Justin whispered.

"No," Kate said, shaking her head, her eyes filling with tears. "We were good, Justin. But we were always heading in different directions. Just like we are now."

"You're making it different," he said.

"Justin," Kate said quietly, standing on her toes and kissing him on the cheek. "I'll always love you. Always. But we don't want the same life."

"I guess Tosh does," Justin said bitterly.

"Yes," Kate answered, "I believe Tosh does."

Justin snatched the wet stick that Mooch was chewing on and hurled it out into the bay. Mooch leapt up and jumped in after it.

"Good boy, Mooch," Justin called. "Good dog."

Justin was ignoring her, and Kate suddenly felt as though she didn't exist.

"Justin—" she said, touching him lightly on the arm.

But he flinched and wouldn't look at her.

"If that's what you've come to tell me," he said, "then I heard you. I'd appreciate it if you would leave now."

Kate winced. The coldness in his voice went right to her heart. *You can't have it both ways, Kate,* she told herself. *You can't reject him and still want him to love you and be your friend.*

"Okay," she said softly. "I'm leaving."

Justin didn't answer, and finally she turned and walked away. She heard the creak of the dock boards below her feet, the sloshing of the water against the pilings, the splash of a big dog hitting the surface of the bay behind her, and nothing else.

FOURTEEN

"Another Guinness for my friend," Tosh called to the waitress as she came to the table where he and Connor were sitting. Where he was sitting and Connor was slouching, actually. They hadn't quite made it until noon, but it was close. Tosh was sitting back in his chair, surveying the boardwalk and the beach. Connor was staring at his empty glass.

Tosh glanced over and shook his head. "You're a picture of gloom," he said to Connor, "if you don't mind my saying."

"It's all a part of the Irish tradition," Connor replied. "I'm a would-be poet taking a closer look at my own despair."

"Oh wow," a female voice said from behind them. "That sounded so amazing."

Connor and Tosh turned at the same time.

151

The blond-haired girl behind them smiled sweetly at Connor. "Are you really a poet?" she asked breathlessly.

Connor's jaw had dropped, but nothing was coming out of his opened mouth.

"Of course he is," Tosh said smoothly.

The girl turned to him, her eyes wide. "And where is he from?"

"He's Irish," Tosh said. "Like all of the important writers of history."

"They were all Irish?" she said, turning back to Connor.

"Sure," Connor finally answered. "And they were all related to me, too. All the important poets of history."

"Wow," she breathed. "I just *love* your accent. Listen," she said, looking at Connor and Tosh, "I have a friend over at another table. Do you think we could join you?"

"Sure," Connor replied, "but you'd probably better tell your friend that my friend here is taken—"

"—in easily by beautiful women," Tosh interrupted, "so ask her not to toy with me too much. I'm very sensitive." He smiled.

"Okay." The girl giggled. "I'll go get her, and we'll be right over." She turned away, and Connor looked at Tosh quizzically.

"No reason to ruin a poor girl's whole day before it's even started," Tosh laughed. "Hold the fort while I go make a call."

Connor smiled stiffly.

"Kate," Chelsea yelled, the phone in her hand, "there's a call for you. I think it's Tosh."

"Got it," Kate said as she grabbed the phone upstairs. She waited for a click as Chelsea hung up. "Hello, Tosh?"

"Hey, babe," Tosh's voice came over the line. "How are you?"

"I'm good," Kate assured him. "Where are you?"

"You'll never believe this, but I ran into an old high-school friend here on the boardwalk," Tosh said excitedly. "It was really a surprise. We used to play basketball together. That was a *long* time ago." He laughed. "Anyway, Kate," he explained, "I wanted to call because it's his last day here, and I said I'd spend the afternoon with him. He'll probably want to go out later, too. You know, couple of guys, sit around and have a few drinks together, that kind of thing. Is it okay, Kate?" Tosh asked worriedly. "I mean, I said yes already, but I can change it if you want. You know how I hate to be away from you."

Kate laughed. "Of course it's okay," she said. "Listen, there's something I wanted to tell you."

"Yes?"

"I had a talk with Justin today," Kate said.

153

"Oh, you did," Tosh said flatly.

"You don't understand," Kate said. "I told him it was over between us. I told him that you and I have a commitment to each other."

"You did?" Tosh said happily. "You know I didn't want to push you—"

"Tosh," Kate said, cutting him off. "You don't have to say anything. I know how you feel. How you must have felt. But it's okay now. I love you."

He sighed deeply. "And I love you, Kate."

Tosh hung up the phone and smiled. "Good, Kate," he whispered, and then walked back toward the table by the beach where Connor was sitting with two very lovely girls.

"Hello, ladies," he said as he lowered himself into his chair. "You're so beautiful, I'm afraid you're blinding me. Are there really two of you?"

They giggled and nodded.

"Oh." Tosh sighed, and smiled. "Well, women as lovely as you shouldn't do this."

"Do what?" they asked.

"Travel in pairs. It's really almost," Tosh paused, "too much for a mere mortal man to handle."

Kate carefully hung up the phone. She hadn't felt very good after speaking to Justin that morning. But she'd decided that all she needed to do was tell Tosh and everything would be all right.

154

As soon as I tell Tosh, she'd thought, *then it will all be put to rest and we will be able to move on.*

But now she had told him. And she didn't feel any better. In fact, something felt terrible.

Come on, Kate, she said to herself. *Shake it off. Of course you feel bad. You love Justin and you hate to see him hurt. But you also love Tosh. And it's not possible to make everybody happy,* she finished.

What about yourself? a voice in her head said.

"I am happy," she whispered fiercely.

Are you? the voice asked. Kate shook away the question—and the answer—and went downstairs.

She found Chelsea on her way out of the kitchen, her fingers and shorts covered in colored chalk dust.

"How's the drawing going?" Kate asked.

"Great," Chelsea said, her eyes full of excitement. "I think they're really good. I'd love you to look at them later."

"I'd be glad to—" Kate started. She was cut off by the sound of the front door slamming, and both she and Chelsea jumped in surprise.

"Marta," Chelsea smiled, "I'm sure that door was in your way, but that's basically what it's there for. Are you okay?"

"Fine," Marta said angrily. "I'm fine. Do you

stand here and ask everyone that question when they come home, or just the cripples?"

Chelsea and Kate looked at each other, their eyebrows raised. Then they each stepped back as Marta rolled swiftly between them to her chair lift.

"You didn't see Dominic today?" Kate asked, trying to guess at the source of Marta's anger.

"Oh, I saw him," Marta snapped as she whirled her chair around and backed into the lift. "I definitely saw him. But I'm not going to see him anymore." Then she jabbed at the button and disappeared downstairs. The last thing Kate saw was her face sinking out of sight, black with anger and confusion. And sadness.

"Wow," Kate breathed softly. "She sure is upset about something."

"You don't think she really thinks that's how I feel about her, do you?" Chelsea asked worriedly. "I mean, thinking of her as a cripple?"

"Chelsea, she's mad at something, or someone," Kate said. "That's for sure. It's not you, though. We were just standing in the wrong place at the wrong time."

"I hope you're right," Chelsea said sadly. "Anyway, I've got to get upstairs and finish my work. I'll let you know when I'm done so you can come and see them, okay?"

Kate nodded and went into the kitchen.

"I heard that from here," Grace said. She and David were at the counter making sandwiches. "I'm glad I wasn't any closer. What's wrong with Marta?"

"I don't know," Kate answered. "But it doesn't look like she knows either." Kate looked at the debris of bread, sandwich meat, lettuce, tomato, mustard, and mayonnaise on the counter. "You look like you're making lunch for an entire team," Kate gasped. "You haven't signed up as a den mother too, have you, Grace?"

"No," David said, laughing. "This is all for me. I have quite an appetite in the best of circumstances, and this afternoon Grace is going on her first solo flight." David winked and leaned closer to Kate. "I get even hungrier when I'm nervous, so she's just planning ahead. She thinks if she gives me something to do, like eating ten sandwiches, I'm not going to notice that she's flying the plane."

"I heard that," Grace said, swatting him on the arm. "Are you saying you don't think I'm ready?"

"Oh, you're ready, all right," David said, rolling his eyes. "And besides, I'd never dare be the one to tell you otherwise."

Grace raised the spatula to hit him again, but David grabbed her and pulled her to him for a long kiss. Then he stepped away, but kept his arm around her as Grace began wrapping all the sandwiches.

"Don't bother putting that stuff away," Kate said. "I'll make myself something since it's out."

"You can make me something too while you're at it," Bo said, rolling into the kitchen on his skateboard. Grace and Kate glared at him, and he got off and picked it up. Roan wandered in behind him.

"I thought you said we could go *out* for lunch," Roan whined.

"Did you guys have fun last night?" Grace asked.

"Yeah," Bo answered. "First we went to the boardwalk, and Roan won a horse in one of the games—"

"And after that we had *fun*," Roan interrupted. "You want to know everything we did? Who we talked to? What time we came home? You know, your brother's not a baby," Roan said casually. "And you're not his mom."

Kate saw Grace's shoulders tense.

"It's all right, Roan," Bo said. "She's just asking. No big deal."

Roan tugged on Bo's sleeve. "Let's get out of here and go to lunch. It *is* my *only* day off," Roan said loudly.

"Do you need any money, Bo?" Grace asked him, wiping her hands off and reaching for her purse.

"No, that's okay," Roan said quickly. "We've

got some, right, Bo? Come on." She grabbed him and pulled him out of the kitchen.

Kate listened to the front door close. "I hope you don't mind my asking," she said.

"I might," Grace snapped.

"Don't take it out on her, Grace," David said.

"Sorry," Grace apologized. "You just saw why I'm tightly strung right now."

"That's actually what I was going to ask you about," Kate said. "I know why you've given Roan a place to stay and a job, and I really do think it's admirable. But what are you going to do about her when the summer's over?"

Grace sighed and pushed her hair back.

"Kate, you know how I always hate to admit it, but our minds sometimes do think alike." She smiled sadly. "That's the question I've been asking myself for a while now. And I really don't know the answer."

FIFTEEN

"Oh, I know this one, I know this one!" Tracy squealed. Or was it Tricia? Connor tried but he couldn't remember which was which.

"How can you be so beautiful and so smart?" Tosh was asking.

How can you be so inane? Connor was thinking.

It turned out the girls weren't related, although they looked nearly identical.

"That's okay." Tosh had smiled. "I'm sure you still borrow each other's clothes, right?"

"Yes," they'd said in chorus.

"So you're practically sisters." He'd laughed.

That had been the tone of most of the day's conversation. Connor's head was pounding. Even his arguments with Chelsea had been more intelligent than this. *What am I doing here?* he asked himself. This was the kind of experience that could turn a man off women forever. *You'd better speak for yourself,* Connor thought, looking over at Tosh. *His interest isn't waning in the least.*

"I'm sorry I have to leave," Connor said suddenly, pushing his chair away from the table and standing. "I've got some more important work to get back to." *Like organizing my toothpicks,* he thought. *Or folding my underwear. Or separating the recyclables.*

"Are you going home to write?" Tricia and Tracy asked in unison.

"Of course he is," Tosh replied. "After spending time with you two lovely women, I'm sure he's so full of inspiration that he's about to burst, if you know what I mean."

The girls giggled and blushed.

"Cheerio," Connor said, and left. Five feet away from the table, he started to feel better. Perhaps it wasn't a headache after all. But then he heard Tosh's laughter behind him, and he started to feel sick again.

Connor was still muttering to himself by the time he got home.

"Low," he was saying as he opened the door to his apartment. "Even in my book. What to do? Don't know. Tell? Not tell? Aren't I a friend? None of my business. I'd want to know . . ."

162

"Are you okay?" Justin asked from the couch. "You sure you have the right apartment? Irish fellow. Wiseass. Basically harmless. Talks to others, not to himself?"

"Hmm, yeah," Connor mumbled. "That's him all right."

Justin skeptically took in Connor's appearance: skin flushed from the beer and the sun, hair standing on end, eyes darting. "You look like you've gotten a few too many rays."

Connor ran his hand through his hair and looked at himself in the small mirror by the door.

"I do look on fire, don't I?" he agreed.

"What are you mumbling about?" Justin asked. "You sounded like you and you were having a pretty intense conversation."

"Oh," Connor said. "I was just wrestling with some of the larger questions about life. You know, truth, liberty, the pursuit of happiness," he faltered.

Connor sighed. He wanted to tell someone about Tosh. The guy was a snake! But was Justin the right person to confide in? If only Chelsea were here, Connor thought angrily. He could tell her and she'd know what to do. She was Kate's best friend. She would know whether to tell her or not.

Talking to Chelsea, though, was about as likely as finding out that Tricia and Tracy were

163

rocket scientists working for NASA. Definitely not something to bet money on.

How could he stand it? Connor thought. *How could Tosh enjoy being with those bimbos when he could be with Kate instead? Someone who was beautiful and smart. And someone he was living with! Well,* Connor reminded himself, *you're married and it didn't stop you from sitting there.*

Justin shook his head and put down his glass of juice. Just then Connor whizzed past, taking the glass with him. Justin reached for the boating magazine he'd been reading, but Connor grabbed that, too.

"Hey, Connor," Justin exploded. "What's the deal?"

"What? Why?" Connor asked.

"That's what I'm asking you." Justin was pointing at Connor's arms.

Connor looked down. His hands were full. While he'd been thinking, he had walked around the apartment picking things up. Newspaper, an empty pizza box, a few beer bottles, a glass half-full of juice, a magazine.

"Just tidying, I guess," Connor explained. "It's good to keep a tidy home. A tidy home's a healthy home."

"I can live with that," Justin said, getting up and walking over to him. "But I'm still drinking

164

this," Justin said as he pried the juice glass from Connor's arm, "and I'm still reading that." He snatched the magazine from Connor's fingers.

"Sorry, mate. I'm trying to work something out," Connor said.

"I could see that when you came in," Justin commented.

Connor sighed and went into the kitchen to empty the load in his arms. He came back and sank into his chair.

"I know something about something and I don't know what to do about it," Connor said in a rush.

Justin nodded. "Now I understand," he said mockingly. "But really, you don't have to give me *all* of the details. The important ones will do."

"It's about Kate," Connor said, sighing. "And Tosh."

Justin's face stayed blank. He waited.

"I was with him today. Man, he is so smooth," Connor said. "He has a look or a word for every woman who passes. I felt like I was back with my football mates at home."

"Well," Justin said slowly, "a lot of guys look."

"That's the problem," Connor said. "He doesn't just look. I left him with *two* women, and he was putting the moves on *both* of them. I know he called Kate, and I don't know what he told her, but he told those girls he was free for the whole evening. This guy's a snake," Connor said. "And Kate should know."

Justin didn't answer for a long time, but Connor didn't mind. He felt better now that he'd shared the burden with someone. At least it wasn't all his responsibility anymore. And Justin would surely do the right thing, Connor thought. *He's in love with her; he won't let this happen.*

"Don't tell anyone else," Justin finally said.

"What?" Connor asked. "Are you crazy?"

"Connor," Justin said sharply, "listen. She made her choice. And she chose him. I'm not going to use sleazy tactics to get her back."

"I didn't think it was a question of sleazy tactics," Connor argued. "It's more a question of he's lying to her, she's getting hurt, and we know it."

"You're right," Justin agreed. "He is lying to her. And she may very well get hurt. But it's not my job to check up on him. Or to take care of her. Or to make sure she doesn't make mistakes." Justin paused and dropped his head into his hands. His next words were a muffled sigh. "Connor, I love her. But I can't save her from her mistakes when she doesn't think she's capable of making them. Maybe she needs to realize that she is."

"Well, here we go," Grace said. "Please make sure all carry-on items, like those sandwiches, are safely and securely stowed in the overhead compartment or below the seat in front of you."

"Or in my stomach," David replied.

Grace and David were strapped into the cockpit of his Cessna, and Grace was checking the multitude of dials and switches on the dashboard of the little plane.

"I remember everything, don't I?" Grace asked, suddenly nervous.

David laughed. "Back at the house you were beating me with kitchenware. Now you're not quite so certain, hmm?" David smiled and reached out and touched her arm. They were talking to each other through their headsets. "Don't worry," he said. "I trust you. And besides, I'm right here. If you need any help, if you have a question, I'm here." He grabbed her hand and squeezed her fingers.

Grace nodded and double-checked all the gauges.

"Okay," she said, looking at the blue sky ahead and above her. "Ready or not, here I come." The plane accelerated, and the engine roared. The joystick buzzed in Grace's hands. The white hash marks before her became a solid line, and the scrub trees bordering the runway turned into a green blur. Grace gently pulled back on the joystick and the nose of the small plane rose into the air.

"Nice lift-off," David said, nodding.

Grace smiled. They were up and circling over the ocean. So much power in her hands.

"It's almost overwhelming," she sighed into her headset. "I'd almost forgotten."

David nodded thoughtfully. "It's only overwhelming if it goes to your head," he said softly. "The trouble comes when you think you can always control the plane. When you think you can make it do whatever you want. The relationship of plane to sky, like other relationships, can only take so much direction."

"David," Grace said. "You sound like a zen master. Don't be so obscure. I know you're talking about something other than flying."

"I don't want to hit you with it up here," he admitted. "You might feel trapped."

Grace's stomach knotted. Instinctively her heart hardened. "Go ahead," she said coldly. "I can take it. What do you have to say? You planning a trip or something?"

"What?" David's voice over the headset was genuinely confused. "Oh, I see," he said suddenly. "Grace." His hand reached out and covered hers. "I wasn't trying to tell you anything about us. I was talking about Roan."

Grace sighed. She hadn't realized how tense she had gotten in the last few moments.

"I guess I'm always thinking—"

"I know what you were thinking," David said, his voice soft in her ears. "I'm not planning on taking a trip anywhere without you."

"Okay," she said. "What about Roan?"

"Did you notice this morning that she seemed a little hazy?" he asked.

"I thought maybe she'd just woken up," Grace tried.

"Come on, Grace," David said. "I can tell from your voice that you know what I'm thinking. I think she's getting high. And I'm sure she's drinking. What are you going to do about it?"

"I don't know," Grace admitted. "I guess I was waiting for a good opportunity to talk with her."

"Grace," David said, still holding her hand. "You're desperate to turn her into another Grace. Another success story. I can see why."

"It's not that," Grace said. "I think maybe I can help her."

"Grace, you don't have a debt to pay, you know."

"Who says I don't?" she shot back.

"You think you can be the mother you never had—" David began.

"No!" Grace interrupted. "That's not what I think. Life's not always a Psych 101 class, you know. All I think is that I can help."

"You can't save her, Grace," David said. "You of all people should know that by now. People

169

like Roan can only save themselves in the end."

"Why does it always have to be like that?" Grace demanded.

"Why can't we, Bo and I, get her to see where drugs and booze will lead her?"

"That's my other point, Grace," David said softly. "What about Bo? You talk like he's your partner, not the little brother who doesn't have your experience. The little brother who has just lost his mother. Who may be more tempted than you are. What if it goes the other way, Grace?" David asked.

Grace looked out at the clouds that surrounded them, the blue emptiness and freedom of the sky.

"What if, rather than Bo helping to pull out Roan, she ends up dragging him in?"

"I hadn't really thought of that," Grace admitted.

"I think you'd better," David advised. "For both of their sakes."

For a moment the vast sky around her seemed to Grace as small as the land they'd left below. She could only fly for so long. Eventually she'd have to turn the plane around and go back home. And she still wasn't sure what she would do when she got there.

"It's him," Connor said when he heard the knock at the door. "It's Tosh. He knows I've told you. He's come here to swear me to secrecy or kill me."

"Connor," Justin sighed, "Tosh is a political science major. A thinker. Not a fighter."

Connor went to the door and looked through the peephole.

"Oh, Lord," he said. "It's a big black man. Do you think it could be another of Chelsea's relatives?" Connor remembered how last summer her family had arrived in a limousine, dragging along their lawyer, prepared to pay him off or deport him so that he wouldn't marry their daughter. Somehow they had been convinced that he and Chelsea loved each other. But by now they probably knew she'd left him.

"They've sent a cousin to kill me," he whispered.

The man outside knocked again.

"Connor, open the door," Justin demanded. "Her family has all those Washington connections. They probably have access to the best assassins in the country. If they're going to kill you, you won't see it coming."

"Thanks for the comforting thought," Connor gulped. Then he opened the door.

"Connor Riordan?" the man asked. "Do I have the right apartment?"

Connor nodded. "That's me," he said.

"Listen, I'm sorry I came to your house." The man smiled.

"I hope I'm not intruding too much. I've just got a deadline I'm trying to beat."

"Please," Connor said, "come in."

"I stopped by the newspaper to see if they could give me any leads," the man said as he stepped inside, "and they sent me here. I run an advertising agency," he explained, "and I'm looking for a good copywriter. A new voice. A sense of humor."

"He's a new voice all right," Justin said from the couch, "and he's definitely got a sense of humor. Paranoid humor, that is."

"Ha ha." Connor chuckled nervously. "Don't mind him. He used to be a lifeguard, but now, lucky me, he seems to be venturing into a brand-new line of work: trying to bury me alive." He turned to Justin and gave him a nasty sneer.

"If you can give me a few moments," the man said, "I'll tell you what I'm looking for right now. Tell you what projects I'm working on. Then you can tell me if you're interested, okay?"

"Okay," Connor agreed.

The man held out a hand and Connor gripped it. "Good," the man said. "I'm happy to meet you. The name's Paul."

SIXTEEN

It was early, and Justin was out on the boardwalk. The sun was just coming up over the ocean. He was wearing a pair of shorts and his running shoes. Now that he wasn't lifeguarding, he figured that he'd better do something to keep himself in shape. He was bent over stretching when between his legs he saw the flash of sunlight on metal. He stood up in time to see Marta roll by.

"Hey," he called, jogging up beside her. "What are you doing out so early?"

Marta looked up and smiled weakly at him.

"I'm exercising," she replied. "I like to do it early in the morning; otherwise there's not enough room for me out here." She nodded down at her chair.

"Good thinking," Justin agreed. "Wouldn't

want you running over any kids in a crowd."

Marta didn't laugh. "Are you running?" she asked curtly. "I'll race you to the end."

"Are you challenging me?" Justin smiled widely.

"Competition is good for the soul, I've heard," Marta commented, squinting into the sunlight.

"If you put it that way, I don't think I can refuse," Justin said, looking at Marta's face, which was drawn and sullen.

"Good." Marta nodded. Then she screamed, "Go!" and she was off down the boardwalk like a shot, her strong arms pumping at the wheels of her chair.

"What the—?" Justin stood still for only a moment, and then he took off after her.

Marta could hear Justin breathing behind her, but she didn't dare turn her head to see how close he was. She knew he was in great shape. One look at that half-clothed body and *anybody* could see what great shape he was in.

But she was fueled by some unknown energy. This morning, when she'd woken up, she had felt it coursing through her body. At least the upper half of her body. She'd been full of so much pent-up energy that she could hardly hold her hand steady long enough to brush her teeth. She'd almost attacked herself with her toothbrush.

And now her muscles were burning as she

fell into her rhythm, rocking back and forth in the seat of her wheelchair, pushing herself forward, faster and faster.

Buildings flew past in a blur. She felt that perhaps she would just take off at any moment. How wonderful that would be, she thought, if her heavy metal chair could lift off the ground and carry her into the sky. Weightless. Unburdened. No more Ocean City, wheelchair, Dominic.

Marta sat up suddenly. Her arms stopped pushing at the wheels of her chair. She was moving fast and her hair streamed out behind her, but she slowed quickly. As she coasted to a stop, she heard Justin running up behind her. He had been pretty far behind, actually, and by the time he reached her, he had slowed down too.

They were both breathing heavily.

"Wow," Justin barely managed to say as he struggled to catch his breath. "You're amazing." He bent over at the waist and hung still for a moment. Then he stood up and looked at her.

"Remind me never to take you up on a challenge again in this lifetime," he said, panting.

Marta smiled but didn't answer. Her shirt stuck to her back and her chest. Her eyes were watery, but she wasn't sure if it was sweat, or the sting of the salt air, or something else.

"Marta," Justin asked, coming forward and putting a hand on her shoulder. "Are you okay?"

She nodded. "Yes," she said, then shook her head. "No."

"Do you want to talk about it?" Justin offered. "I seem to be on the receiving end of lots of confessions lately. I must be pretty good at it by now," he said, shrugging his shoulders. "Up to you."

Marta rolled over to the edge of the boardwalk, and Justin sat down beside her.

"Did you meet Dominic?" she asked.

"No," Justin said. "Never met him, but Connor mentioned him to me. He's the guy you've been seeing lately, right? From your hometown? The one who makes you break out in song?"

"Not anymore," Marta said curtly. "We won't be seeing each other again."

"Oh," Justin said. "Sorry."

"You don't have to be sorry," Marta replied. "It was my decision. Not like you and Kate."

"What about me and Kate?" Justin asked.

"Look, Tosh is living in Grace's house," Marta said matter-of-factly, "and you're living with Connor. It's obvious that you aren't seeing each other anymore, and I doubt that it's your choice."

"Thanks for the kid gloves," Justin said. "Why don't you think it's my choice?" he asked. "Do I look that pathetic?"

Marta looked at him slowly. "You've never looked pathetic, Justin," she said in a low voice. "You know that."

She was surprised to see Justin blush. "It's just that I know you were in love with her. And I saw the look on your face that first day you were back, when Tosh came in," she explained. "I figured your feelings for her hadn't changed. But hers obviously have."

Justin winced. "Marta, you really have a way with words, don't you? If you were anybody else, I'd be furious with you."

"But you wouldn't dare hit me because I'm in a wheelchair?" she added sarcastically.

"No," Justin said, looking up at her face. "Because I hope I know you well enough to realize that you're just being honest. You're not trying to hurt me." He paused. "Are you?"

Marta smiled back at him. "No, I'm not trying. But I'm probably not completely innocent," she admitted. "I'm angry, and I guess I wouldn't mind if I made you angry also. It's the natural thing for most people to do when they're in pain—to make others hurt too."

"Well," said Justin slowly. "You said your situation was different from mine. How so? Don't you love Dominic?"

"I did. But I can't see him anymore," Marta said, "although it's not because of anyone else."

"Why?" Justin asked. "Did he do something to you?"

Marta nodded. "A long time ago," she said. "I

thought he was a different person then." Marta shook her head. "I thought it didn't matter. But I was wrong."

"What did he do?" Justin's voice was hardly a whisper.

"He shot me." Marta's voice floated back to him. "He put me here," she said, her hands tapping the armrests, "in this chair."

"He *what*?" Justin leaped up. "I can't believe you're sitting there so calmly," he said, stalking around her.

"He was in a gang back then," Marta explained. "He didn't know me. It was an accident."

"An accident?"

"Well," Marta admitted, "he was trying to shoot someone else, but I just happened to get in the way."

"Did he go to jail?" Justin asked.

"No," Marta admitted. "They never found out who did it."

"And he came here looking for you?"

"Yes," she said. "He changed his life. He went back to school. He came to find me to apologize. To do whatever he could to try and make it up to me, I guess." She sighed. "I fell in love with him before he told me who he was."

Justin winced. "That was pretty sneaky," he said.

"Maybe," Marta agreed. "It seems beside the

point now, though. I thought it didn't matter. I thought I could forgive him. But I was wrong. I can't tell him everything is all right just because he finally started feeling guilty. He made a mistake," Marta said. "And now he'll have to pay for it. It's not my responsibility to take care of his emotions. I have to take care of my own."

Justin smiled sadly. "Perhaps we have more in common than you think," he said, reaching out and giving her shoulder a squeeze. He ran his other hand through his hair and looked behind them at the boardwalk.

"Since I lost the race," he started.

"We never finished it," Marta corrected.

"You're right." Justin smiled. "But since I was definitely losing, and if you hadn't stopped you would probably have beaten me by a half mile at least, I'll pay for the movie."

"What movie?" Marta said, looking at him suspiciously.

"The movie I'm going to take you to tonight," Justin replied.

Marta smiled. "Oh, that movie."

"Come on, champ," Justin said, turning away from her. "I'll walk you home."

Marta laughed, surprised for the first time in a long time. "Hey," she called, rolling after him, "you aren't even going to offer to help me?"

"Me?" Justin yelled back over his shoulder.

179

"Help you? That's a laugh, coming from the woman who just kicked my ass all the way down the boardwalk."

"There you go," Chelsea said, dropping her drawings onto the desk in Paul's office. "I hope you don't mind that they're early."

Paul smiled and pulled the three sheets of paper from the portfolio. "Mind?" he asked. "Do I mind that you're early?" He laughed loudly. "Chelsea, have I told you that I've been looking for you all my life? Oh, come to think of it, I already have, and although that didn't impress you, you *still* got these to me ahead of schedule."

Chelsea blushed at his reference to their unsuccessful date a few nights before.

Paul laid out the three drawings on his desk and walked around them. "Hmmm," he said, nodding. "Hmmm."

"'Hmmm'?" Chelsea asked. "Is 'hmmm' a good thing? That's a description my teachers never used."

Paul looked up at her, his eyes twinkling. "Is it a good thing? I'm sorry, Chelsea. 'Hmmm' is a very good thing. Let me translate." He came around the desk and took her hand and led her to his desk. "'Hmmm' means, 'Yes, these are fantastic. Bold colors, great design, eye-catching, with vision and a sense of humor.' I told you that

I thought you were capable of all that the first day I met you on the beach. I didn't think I'd be lucky enough to get it all on your first assignment, though."

Chelsea looked down at her work. The design was actually very similar to what she'd been doing on the beach when Paul had met her: in each picture, the composition centered around two people in a crowd. Two people who didn't really seem to belong at the beach at all. And around them were the bright lights of the neon signs on the boardwalk, and a mass of moving bodies, all tan and young and happy.

In one picture the man and woman were both wearing big hats, shorts and knee socks, and looking around them nervously. In another, they were in bathing suits, but very pale and walking under an enormous parasol. The third picture was of the couple she had already sketched. They wore their gaudy silk robes and their faces were full of suspicion.

"I really like your vision," Paul said. "Your pictures focus on people who would never use the product we want to sell, and you show them uncomfortable and lost in their surroundings. It targets our audience, the young happy tan people around them, and says, 'Hey, you aren't those two people in the middle. You're part of the comfortable group. You enjoy the beach, and you use our suntan lotion.' Isn't that what you were thinking?" Paul turned to her.

Chelsea's jaw had dropped. "Uh," she said, "hmmm, yes, I guess so." She shook her head and blushed. "Honestly, Paul, I don't know if I worked it out that fully. It was more of an instinct, really."

Paul smiled at her discomfort. "That's what I thought, Chelsea," he said. "With great artists, it's almost always instinct."

"Next time I'll just take 'hmmm' when I get it," she said.

"That's probably a good idea," Paul agreed. "Believe me, if the art won't work, I'll know it right away, and you'll hear that long before you hear another 'hmmm,' okay?"

"Okay," Chelsea said. "But tell me again, just now, that you like these?"

Paul hugged her quickly. "They're great, Chelsea. I knew they would be. Listen, there's more work here for you if you want it. I've actually just taken on a new client. And I've found a very bright young copywriter." He paused and gave her a searching look, and then nodded to himself. "I'd like you to get together with him soon, to start work for this new client. It's a major seafood restaurant chain with outlets along the entire eastern seaboard," he explained, "so there's more to think about than the local wildlife here in Ocean City. I'll want you two to try and plan out an entire campaign strategy together. Words and images."

"Wow," Chelsea breathed. "You really believe in me," she said, half questioningly.

"I do believe in you." Paul smiled. "And I hope that you two will be able to come up with something very special."

"We will," Chelsea assured him. "I'm sure we will."

SEVENTEEN

"So how was yesterday?" Chelsea asked as they all sat in the downstairs rec room. "Are you ready to open your own rival flying school?"

"It was a triumph," Grace acknowledged.

"That means you can call her Ace," David said, laughing, as he pulled Grace down beside him onto the soft couch.

"What about you?" Kate asked Chelsea. "How's the advertising world coming?"

"He liked my work." Chelsea smiled. "And he's giving me more. A big seafood restaurant chain."

"Wow," David said.

Chelsea nodded.

"That's amazing!" Kate yelped. "He must have been really impressed."

"He wants us to come up with an entire ad campaign."

"Us?" David asked, his face lighting up with excitement.

"Not 'us' as in us here at the house." Chelsea laughed. "Us as in me and the copywriter he hired."

"Oh," David said dejectedly.

"But we can still help," Grace said, ruffling David's hair.

"How about 'Where's the fish?'" Kate suggested.

"Fish," David said. "It's what's for dinner."

"Fish, America's favorite," Grace added.

"The scallops generation."

"Scrod is it!"

"Shrimp and clams—melt in your mouth, not in your hands."

"Just tuna it!"

"Okay," Grace interrupted. "Who's hungry for dinner?"

"I'll order," Chelsea said, grabbing the phone. "Two large pies with everything?"

There was silence for a moment.

"Okay, okay." Grace sighed. "My suggestion. I'll pay."

Grace went to search for her wallet but couldn't find it. "I must have left it in my coat," she said to herself and ran up the stairs to her room. Her coat pockets were empty. She looked on the floor, under the chair, in the bathroom. She was about to leave when she saw her wallet lying behind the phone on the table by her bed.

"Strange," she said as she grabbed it and went for the door. Then she opened her wallet and stopped. It was empty.

For a moment all she felt was shock. And disbelief. Then she remembered the other times lately when she was sure she'd had cash only to find her wallet empty.

"I am *not* this careless," she said vehemently. Her mind was reeling. "You're a fool, Grace Caywood," she said to herself. "A fool."

She passed everyone on the main floor. Kate was coming from the kitchen with a stack of paper plates, three small candles, and the tacky blue-and-red table globes Grace had bought in her first household shopping spree.

"We thought we'd eat on the deck," Chelsea explained, following Kate with napkins and silverware.

Grace nodded and smiled mechanically. "See you there in a minute," she said. She started down the other flight of steps to the bottom floor and saw David coming up.

"Are you coming outside, Grace?" he asked.

"Mmm-hmm," she nodded, brushing past him. "See you there in a minute."

Grace crossed to the door of Roan's room. A bedroom with a view of the ocean. A bedroom

187

on the beach. A bedroom in a nice house. *In my house,* Grace fumed.

"Fool," she whispered. "You are about to do something completely unethical," she told herself. "But you have been taken for a fool." Grace put her hand on the doorknob.

"Who's a fool, Grace?" David's voice was right behind her. Grace snatched her hand from Roan's door and spun around.

"I'm a fool," she hissed.

"Why, Grace. What are you doing?" he asked.

"You were right, David," Grace said coldly. "I'm so blinded by seeing myself, I can't even see who she is."

"Roan?"

"Yes," Grace whispered. "She's a goddamn bitch, and a little thief on top of it, and Lord knows what else. But I'm going to find out, and you can't stop me."

"I wouldn't try to stop you, Grace," he said. "It is your house."

Grace turned, opened the door, and stepped inside.

The room was a mess. *She's a mess,* Grace thought. Clothes were scattered around the floor. There was a small china plate from the cupboard upstairs sitting on the windowsill. There were burn spots, and a few crumpled cigarette butts. Grace ran her hands lightly over the table, looking around. Somewhere inside her, the room seemed familiar, as if she had lived here herself. *You have,* she reminded herself. *You have lived this life, exactly.* Grace went to the bed, lifted the blankets, and peered underneath. She caught her breath. Bottle caps gathering dust. Bottles. On their sides. Mostly empty. Two in the back, near the head of the bed standing upright with an inch or so of amber liquid still in each.

Grace stood quickly and went to the closet. She found a bottle in the back, hidden behind a pair of scruffy boots. She moved to the dresser, pulling open drawers, her fingers pushing quickly through the contents. Grace's hand stopped on something. A new lacy camisole she had bought herself last week and thought she'd lost in the wash. Then she looked closer and recognized a bright pink tank top that she thought was probably Chelsea's. A small pair of white shorts that could belong to Marta. Kate's wool hiking socks.

There was a pair of jeans on the floor. The cuffs were dark. Grace bent down and felt them. Wet. She smelled her fingers. Saltwater. She grabbed the pants and felt around the pockets. One was full. She reached in and pulled out a small plastic bag with two joints in it and a few crumpled pieces of damp green paper. She unfolded two twenty-dollar bills.

"Grace?" David's voice came from the doorway as he stepped inside.

Grace turned and held out her shaking hands. She was so angry, she thought she might explode. Angry, and something else, she thought, conscious of David blurring before her as her eyes filled with tears. She was angry, and she was hurt. Hurt because she felt she'd been betrayed.

"Are you okay?" David's voice was full of concern.

"I'm fine," Grace said, wiping her eyes. "I'm going to forget about this for an hour and have a good dinner. With my friends. And then I'm going to go out and find her—and wring her little neck."

Chelsea heard the front door open and close and turned from the view of the ocean to see Marta heading for her chair lift.

"Marta," she called. "We're having a fancy pizza dinner out here, which Grace is kindly paying for, if you want to join us."

"Oh?" Marta paused. "Who all is out there?" she asked innocently.

"Me and Kate and David and Grace," Chelsea answered.

"That's nice," Marta replied. "Thanks anyway, but I actually have something to do already."

"Hot date?" Chelsea asked.

"No, no," Marta answered as she got into the chair lift. "Just a friend."

Downstairs in her room Marta changed out of the shirt she'd worn at the clinic all day. She quickly brushed out her hair and checked her watch. Justin was coming over in a few minutes and she wanted to do him the favor of being ready. It wouldn't be very comfortable if he had to loiter around *this* house waiting for her, especially when Kate was home.

Marta had offered to meet him outside, or across the street in front of Connor's apartment. But he had quickly said no to that. He was right, of course, and Marta had been embarrassed for suggesting it. Since they definitely weren't going on a date, there was no reason to be sneaking around as if they were.

Still, she thought. She didn't want Kate getting the wrong impression. Which she probably would if Justin came to get Marta and had to wait around for her. It would make the whole evening seem much more formal than it really was.

Marta checked herself in the mirror again and nodded. *Can't do any better,* she thought. Then she put her bag on her lap and rolled herself out of her room, trying to ignore the butterflies in her stomach.

She reached the main floor as Kate went into the kitchen, holding a napkin to her white shirt.

"I'm on a club-soda search. Pizza-sauce stain," Kate cringed. "Food fight outside," she explained with a smile. "Be glad you're going out."

Just then the doorbell rang. Marta grabbed the keys to her van and rolled to the front door.

"Hey, Marta." Justin smiled. "You look great," he said.

"Thanks." Marta smiled. "Are you ready? I thought I'd drive, okay?"

"Fine," Justin answered. There was a burst of laughter from the deck. He glanced up and looked over her shoulder, through the creamy comfortable living room, through the glass doors, out to the deck and the flickering candles. And he paused for a moment, as if he were waiting for something. Then his eyes hardened and he stepped aside to let Marta roll out.

They burst out of the back doors of the movie house laughing hysterically. Justin fell against Marta's wheelchair and spun her around.

"That was definitely the worst film I've ever seen," Marta said, her eyes sparkling. "What was it called, *Horror Movie Number Seventeen*?"

"Wasn't it great?" Justin agreed. "Exactly what we needed. Those were the kind of characters who remind me that I'm not as stupid as I may look." Justin winked.

"Stupid isn't the word that comes to mind when *I* look at you," Marta joked.

Justin caught up to her, and without thinking, they both reached out and grasped each other's hand. They reached her van, and this time, although he still didn't help, Justin waited until she'd gotten herself in before he went around to the passenger-side door.

It was nice, he thought, spending time with her. Marta was so uncomplicated. Everything was out in the open with her, and Justin admired the way she handled herself in her wheelchair. She seemed capable, and accepting, completely at ease with her situation. And she had a great sense of humor about it when strangers started treating her like an invalid.

He hadn't noticed it until she pointed it out to him, but sometimes as soon as people saw her wheelchair, they started speaking louder to her, leaning over into her face as if she were deaf. Or they spoke to her like they were speaking to a five-year-old, as if she could no longer understand English. Or they tried to steer her chair, pointing out things in front of her, "Oh-oh, and there's a person on your right there," as if she must be blind.

"You have an unbelievable tolerance level," Justin told her after dinner. "If I were in your place, I would have probably been in five fistfights by now, and we would never get to the movie."

"In the beginning, I *tried* to get into fistfights," Marta had explained. "Believe me, I wanted to fight the whole world."

"You fought?" Justin asked.

Marta shook her head. "I never could find anyone who was actually willing to raise a hand against me. Tolerance came with time," she stated. "It was hard enough to fight myself, let alone fight everyone else. First I just got tired. Only later did I start to understand why others couldn't be expected to always do the right thing."

Justin was amazed by her. By how much she had overcome. He thought of the problems that were between Kate and himself, and he felt embarrassed by them. It was true, they had each had their share of difficulty and pain; Kate had lost her sister Juliana to suicide, and Justin's father had AIDS. If he wasn't dead already, he most likely would be soon. But death could be mourned. And peace could still be made with ghosts, Justin knew. Kate had made her peace with his ghost, Justin reminded himself. And with him. Well, if that was her decision, he had to accept it. Make his own peace. And move on.

"What deep thoughts are going on behind those eyes?" Marta asked lightly as she maneuvered the huge vehicle smoothly into traffic.

"Oh," Justin looked over at her and smiled, "just thinking about the weather." He shook his head. "Nothing important. Why?"

"Oh," she joked, "just beginning to wonder if it was twelve o'clock and my prince had turned into a mouse again."

"And your chariot a pumpkin?" Justin added.

"I wish," Marta said jokingly. "Then I could bake my wheelchair into a pie and be rid of it forever."

Justin smiled. "No one's ever called me her prince before," he said slowly.

Marta pulled up in front of the old Victorian house.

"Listen," she said, "I had a great time. And I needed one. Thanks."

Justin nodded and reached out and took her hand. "I had a great time too," he said softly, smiling in the darkness. "I'll lose a bet to you anytime."

EIGHTEEN

"Come on, Bo." Roan's voice floated back to him. He heard her twist the cap off the bottle she was carrying and take a drink. "What are you doing back there?" she whined.

They were far down the beach, at the south end of the boardwalk. Roan was heading into the darkness beneath it.

"Why do you like to hang out under here all the time?" Bo asked. "It's creepy as hell."

"Maybe," Roan said. "But it's private. And my privacy is very important to me, you know." She leaned over her shoulder and gazed at him. "Come on, sit down with me. Don't you like looking at the ocean?"

She flopped down onto the sand and leaned back against one of the large wooden pilings. Bo dropped to the sand next to her.

"The stars are beautiful, aren't they?" Roan asked. "I love the sky at night."

There was almost a full moon and the sand glittered in the milky light. Bo could see other couples walking along by the water's edge. Above them the sounds of the amusement park mingled with the screaming and laughter of a hundred people.

Colored lights from the games and rides shone down through the cracks of the boardwalk and fell onto the sand in broken flashing patterns. Bo turned and saw Roan's face lit up by purple and orange bursts. She looked strangely beautiful, like a doll.

Then she bent her head and tried to light the small white joint in her fingers.

"Damn," she muttered. "It's wet."

She flicked the lighter against the end another five times before she finally got it started. Then she took a deep drag. She held her breath, and passed the bottle to Bo.

"Here," Roan said as she exhaled. "It's peppermint. It makes your breath smell nice." She paused and smiled and licked her lips. "It tastes good too."

Bo held the bottle loosely in his hands.

"Go on," Roan urged. "Just smell it. It's yummy. Trust me."

Bo carefully unscrewed the cap and raised

the bottle to his nose and sniffed.

"See," Roan said, nudging him. "I told you so."

Bo quickly licked the top of the bottle. It burned his tongue. Instinctively he squeezed his eyes shut and wrinkled his nose. Roan laughed.

"Oh, you're such a beginner," she squealed, taking another drag off her joint. She turned and exhaled slowly into his face. It was an overpowering sweet smell that clogged his throat. Bo started coughing.

"It's okay," Roan said, reaching out and ruffling his hair. She leaned over to give him a kiss on the cheek and knocked the bottle of schnapps from his hand into his lap.

Roan collapsed into fits of laughter.

Bo wiped himself off and pushed the bottle away into the sand.

"What's so funny?" he said sullenly. He didn't really want Roan to be acting this way, but he wanted to be with her. And it seemed as though being with her meant doing what she wanted to do.

Roan finally caught her breath, took one last drag, and crushed the end of the joint into the sand.

"I'm sorry, Bo-Bo." She giggled. "Am I making you angry?"

He shook his head.

"Good," she sighed, leaning against him.

"Because I don't want you to be mad at me. You're really sweet."

Bo slipped his arm around Roan carefully. He could feel his heart starting to pound, and he hoped she wasn't noticing. Her hair was flashing purple and blond in the darkness. He reached up one hand and stroked it.

"Mmm," Roan sighed, snuggling closer to him. "That's nice. You're so nice to me. And Grace, too," Roan added. "I'm glad she brought me home. And I'm glad you live there."

Roan was high, but she was telling the truth. She slipped her hand under Bo's shirt. She could feel his heart beating in his chest. Knowing that she had that effect on him made her smile. Roan looked up at him.

"You and Grace are both so pretty," she said, looking into his green eyes.

"You're beautiful," Bo said softly, blushing.

Roan smiled and pulled away from him. Then she leaned over and kissed him on the lips.

"You're the first person," Roan whispered to him, pulling away.

"First for what?" Bo asked, opening his eyes.

"The first person I've ever wanted to be with for nothing. For no money, I mean."

Bo looked shocked, and Roan turned away.

"I shouldn't have told you that," she said. "I'm not a slut, you know. I don't sleep with anyone."

She started to cry, and Bo reached out to her.

"I only did it a few times," she whimpered.

"It's all right," he said, holding her tightly. "I don't care."

"When I had no money, you know . . . there were some times when it was bad, really bad. . . . I couldn't always sleep on the street. . . . One night it rained on me, and I got really sick . . . and after that . . . a few times—"

"I don't care," Bo said.

"Can you get me the bottle?" she asked.

He reached over and plucked it from the sand. Roan took the bottle and wiped the sand from the rim. She tipped it back and took a long swallow.

"Share it with me?" she asked, handing it back to Bo.

Grace was sitting in the darkened living room. She checked her watch again. After midnight.

"Where the hell are you, Bo?" she whispered. "You *know* you're not supposed to come home this late."

Chelsea had gone to her room to sketch. Kate and Tosh were out taking a walk on the beach. Marta had come home twenty minutes ago, singing to herself, and gone down to her room. David she had sent home.

"You don't want me to see this, is that it?" he'd asked.

"Maybe," she replied. "Maybe I need to do this alone. You already saw it coming. I was the one who was taken in."

"Grace, do you really think she's that calculating?" David asked.

"I know she's stealing my money. And everyone else's clothes. And I think my brother's spending too much time with her." She paused. "You were right. I can't be her mother. And I can't let her get away with this."

Grace heard the door open and she tensed. She saw them stumble in together, but she couldn't tell who was leaning on whom. She snapped on the light beside her and stood up.

"Bo," she barked.

He looked up and saw her, and his face burned.

"Gracie," he said, and smiled weakly, taking a step forward.

"What are you doing, waiting up for us?" Roan asked. "Is your own love life so uninteresting you need to follow around your little brother?" Roan was trying to sound flippant, but her voice wavered. Grace knew she was afraid.

"Shut up and get over here," Grace said, her voice low.

Bo and Roan parted, and crossed into the living room.

"Don't you talk to me like that," Grace hissed

at Roan. "A year ago I would have taken you outside and beaten the crap out of you. I *may* not do that tonight, but don't think it's because I can't." She leaned over and her eyes bored into Roan's. Grace held her hand up in front of Roan's face, her thumb and finger a half inch apart.

"You are this big to me right now," Grace said.

"Gracie," Bo whined, "please don't talk to her like that. Why are you so mad?"

Grace straightened and went over to him. She smelled him long before she reached him. He reeked of alcohol and smoke.

"You've been smoking," Grace said flatly. "And drinking."

"Lay off him," Roan started, but Grace whirled and cut her off.

"Shut up!" she yelled. "This is between me and *my brother.*"

She looked back at Bo. David was right, she thought, looking at her little brother. She's changing him, and I'm letting her.

"I can't speak to you about this now," Grace said to him, her voice choked.

"Come on, Grace," Bo said, squirming. "I'm sorry, all right. Don't yell at her, please. . . ."

"Bo, dammit, listen to me," Grace's anger broke. She stepped back so that she could see them both. "Your *girlfriend* is a thief, and a liar,"

Grace yelled. "And an alcoholic and an *addict*!"

"I'm not an alcoholic," Roan snapped. "That was you! Don't confuse me with yourself, okay? I don't have your problems."

"Oh, really," Grace said. Then she pulled a bag from behind the couch and emptied it onto the living-room floor. All the bottles from under Roan's bed clinked out onto the carpet, along with all the stolen clothes from Roan's drawer and the plastic bag with Roan's drugs and Grace's money.

"I can't believe you went in my room!" Roan screeched, starting to cry.

"Oh, you can't believe I went into your room, which is part of *my* house. And that's supposed to be worse than you being a drunk, and a thief, and taking my brother out and getting him stoned! Nice try, Roan. This crap is in my house, and you're the one breaking the goddamn law, and we could *all* go to jail for this. Don't you know that!"

Grace turned to Bo.

"Ask her," Grace demanded. "Ask her how much money she's stolen from me since I brought her into my house, gave her food, clothes, and a job."

Bo's mouth opened and closed wordlessly.

"Ask her!" Grace demanded.

"Roan?" Bo said shakily, turning to her.

"I can't believe you," Roan cried at him. "I can't believe after tonight you're treating me like this."

"He's asking you a question, Roan," Grace sneered. "Can't you answer it? Just the truth, that's all. Just a simple question. How much, Roan? Three hundred? Four? I'd say that's pretty good money for only a few weeks' worth of work, wouldn't you?"

"Better money than what you were paying me," Roan shot back.

Bo looked away, his face crumpling.

Grace knew she was hurting him, but he had to see it. He had to know for himself what was going on.

"I guess you're right, Roan," Grace said. "I was ripping you off. Everything I gave you was just crap. A place to live. A job. Well, you don't have to take it anymore," Grace said, her arm sweeping the room. "Lord knows we don't have to take you anymore. I'm not cut out to be your mother and I don't want to be your baby-sitter. And my first obligation is to Bo. My brother, who you've already set out to mess up. Well, forget it," Grace whispered. "You can forget that. Because I won't let that happen."

Grace crossed her arms over her chest and took a deep breath.

"Tomorrow I'm going to call Social

Services. We'll work something out then."

Roan looked down at the pile of clothes and bottles at her feet. Her eye fell on the one full bottle she'd hidden in her closet. Her hand clenched.

"Don't even think about it," Grace whispered, knowing what Roan was looking at.

Roan paused another moment, and then turned and ran from the room. Grace listened to the sound of her feet on the stairs, and the slamming of her door. Then she turned to Bo. She stepped toward him and put her hand out, knowing that he must be hurting. But he flinched away from her, and turned his back.

"Okay, Bo," Grace said. "I sent my message, and you sent yours. Go to bed now."

Grace watched him walk away and disappear into the darkened kitchen. She waited to turn off the light beside her until she heard his door close. And then she sank down onto the carpeted floor, her hands touching the bottles. And she started sobbing.

NINETEEN

Grace was identifying the body. *She's the one in the fancy clothes*, Grace was saying. *She's the one in the birthday suit*, they replied. Then she saw her mother behind them, a party hat slipping off her head. Ellen Caywood's face was blue. A long thin piece of seaweed was hanging from her mouth. *It's my birthday*, she was saying to Grace, *and you didn't get me a thing. Ungrateful.* She turned to go. *Wait, Mother*, Grace called, *I'll get you something before you go in.* Her mother, naked at the water's edge, turned to look at her. *You don't care*, she sighed. *You never cared.* Something hit Grace on the head. *Try this*, Justin said as the cooler fell to her feet. Grace picked it up and went after her mother, but they wouldn't let her pass. *She's the one in the fancy clothes*, they mocked, *she's the one in the birthday suit. You can't do this,* Grace called out to her. *Where else can you live? Who else will take care of you?* They laughed as Grace watched her mother disappear into the ocean.

The door to Grace's bedroom burst open and Bo charged in.

"She's gone!" he screamed.

Grace sat up in bed, immediately awake. Her eyes were open, but the nightmare still clung to her. She looked around wildly.

"She's gone," Bo shouted again. "Are you satisfied now?"

"Who?" Grace cried, her hands at her ears. "Who are you yelling about?"

"Roan," Bo wailed. "She's gone, and you scared her away. I hope you're happy now," he spit out, then turned on his heel and left her room.

Grace got out of bed, wrapped herself quickly in a robe, and hurried downstairs.

Kate, Tosh, Chelsea, and Marta were already in the kitchen.

"What is this," Grace snapped, "a runaway convention?"

"He woke all of us when he found her room empty," Tosh explained. "He wanted to make sure she wasn't in the house before he woke you."

Grace could hear Bo banging around downstairs in Roan's room. She looked around the kitchen, unsure.

"What should I do?" she asked.

"What happened last night?" Kate asked.

Grace sighed and pushed her hair from her face. Her hands were shaking.

"She's really gone?" Grace asked. "Just like that?"

"Grace," Chelsea pressed, "what happened?"

"She's been stealing," Grace whispered. "Money. Lots of money, from me—and other things, from all of you. Anything you've been missing for a while," Grace said distractedly, "she had it."

Grace could tell from the way they were looking at one another that each of them had thought of a few things they hadn't been able to find.

"And she's been drinking." Grace's breath caught in her throat. "Her room was like the storeroom of a bar. And she's with Bo all the time. Last night they were smoking."

"Cigarettes?" Tosh asked.

Grace shook her head. "I'm not that ridiculous," she snapped. "No, not cigarettes. I wouldn't be happy about that at all, but I'd be much happier than I am now."

Bo came into the kitchen and stopped when he saw them all there. He was carrying a small bag. Full of clothes for Roan, no doubt, Grace surmised. *He looks decked out to be a regular hero,* she said to herself angrily.

Bo looked at Grace quickly, then brushed past

her into his room. He came out a moment later with his skateboard, a jacket, and a backpack.

"What's in there?" Grace asked, pointing at the two bags.

"Things for Roan," he snapped. "And things for me. What do you care anyway?"

"Bo, you can't leave," Grace said. "What are you going to do on your own?"

Bo stopped and looked back at her. "Wow," he said slowly. "You sounded just like Mom then. Remember when she used to say that stuff to you, Grace? Do you? Do you remember what you used to answer?"

Grace went numb.

"I won't repeat it," Bo said, looking around at everyone's silent faces. "I wouldn't want to embarrass you in front of your friends."

"Bo," Grace cried. "How can you be angry at me? She stole from all of us. Look at you! You look like you're going into the jungle. This isn't a rescue mission, Bo. You can't just toss her a bag of clothes like that's going to be enough to save her, to change her whole life! She drinks, Bo. At least you can see that! The last thing we need is another drunk around here."

"That's easy for you to say now," Bo answered, "but maybe you don't remember those days not too long ago when I used to call you up after you'd been drinking. But come to think of it," Bo said sarcastically, "you wouldn't remember that, now would you. You didn't even remember it then. You're such a hypocrite! You said I could always count on you," Bo whispered. "Can I count on you now?"

Grace didn't answer.

Bo shook his head and hiked the backpack onto his shoulder.

"I hear you in here," Bo said. "Telling them you care about me. But it's not true. All you care about is yourself. You may not drink anymore," Bo said, his eyes filling with tears, "but you're still Mom all over again."

Bo turned to leave, then stopped and looked back.

"I care about her, Grace. And I'm going to be with her." He stalked out of the room.

Grace sagged against the counter. "Don't say anything." She lowered her head and raised her hand to block the faces around her. "Please don't say anything right now, okay? I feel terrible, and I need to be alone."

Grace didn't raise her head again until everyone had gone.

Then she left the kitchen and walked through the living room, past the pile of bottles and clothes, and out onto the deck. She stared at the water.

I couldn't have saved you, Mother, Grace

211

thought, *but I should have learned from you.*

"I promised myself I'd never do what you did," Grace whispered. "But he's left me. Just like I left you."

Marta looked across the street hesitantly and then turned her chair toward the boardwalk.

"You're only going to exercise," she said to herself. "It doesn't *mean* anything."

Marta went for an early roll most mornings. It wasn't strange that she was out. *So why does it feel so strange?* Marta asked herself. *Probably because you don't usually go exercising in the hopes of running into a handsome half-naked man who might like you,* she replied.

"Marta." The voice was so unexpected, so soft. She'd thought she'd almost forgotten it until she heard it again, saying her name, and realized that it had been there all the time, lingering, familiar. He stepped from the bushes.

"Marta," he said again, looking into her eyes. He made no move to step closer.

It had been only four days since she'd seen him. And before she could get angry, her hands grabbed the wheels of her chair and began to push her toward him. But then she shook her head, her fists gripping the cool metal rails. She took a breath and leaned back into her chair, away from him.

From the beginning she had been drawn to him. To the dark eyes, to the pain in them. The pain and the mystery. To the soft voice that was an intimate surprise. To his soul.

It's the goddamn Florence Nightingale syndrome, Marta screamed to herself. *Laugh at it. Get over him! Get over your pity, your interest. You never wanted them for yourself.*

"Marta," Dominic said again. "I wanted to see you again. One more time."

She nodded curtly. "You've seen me," she said. "I'm still here. Same as you left me. Me and my chair."

Dominic winced but didn't look away.

"Can we talk?" he asked.

"I came out here to exercise," Marta said. "A person in *my* condition needs to keep to a strict regimen. A person in *my* condition needs to have a lot of drive, to stay healthy and in shape. It's far too easy for someone in *my* position, that is, *sitting* for the *rest* of my life, to let herself go, you know?"

"Where are you going?" he asked softly. "Can I walk you there?"

"You *could*," Marta sneered. "Think about that. In another life, you might have been able to walk *with* me there."

Marta rolled past him toward the boardwalk. He fell into step beside her chair. Marta yearned to let loose, to speed away so that she wouldn't be able to see, from the corner of her eye, the long strides of his legs as he walked next to her. But she forced herself to roll calmly. She didn't want to run away from him. She didn't want to believe he had that power over her.

What does it matter? she thought. *If you can't forgive him, forget him. Like the ocean,* she said as she saw it before her. The waves washed against the shore. Gulls circled and dove for remnants from the night's tides. *Every day the ocean washes away the beach. Every day. What does it care? In fifty years none of it will matter anyway.*

"Marta," he said, "I know it's not easy. I know you're angry. And you have that right. But I want to do something, Marta. I can't just let you say you're angry and give up. I had to try once more."

His hands were deep in his pockets, as if he might find something there. Some answer.

"We're here," Marta said as she rolled up onto the boardwalk, Dominic at her side. "This is where I start."

"If you don't want to see me anymore, I won't argue," Dominic said urgently, stepping in front of her. "I'll leave town and never try to speak to you again. If that's my punishment—"

"What do you think!" she burst out, cutting him off. "What do you think? You think that I can

214

stay with you, spend time with you, knowing what I know? You think I can stand to look at you and realize you're to blame for all of the pain in my life? You didn't just take my legs," Marta cried. "You took my whole life. You took my house, my friends, the place where I grew up, the streets I played on. You took my mother, for God's sake! And you took my father, you ruined him. He thought he was a strong man—a man who could take care of his family. But after you shot me, no one believed that anymore. Not me, for a while, not my mother, ever again. She left him, you know. She left us," Marta gasped. "He's never forgiven himself, and I'm supposed to forgive you because you finally feel a bit guilty?"

"No!" Dominic answered, his voice rising to match hers. "Because I don't feel guilty. I spent the last few years trying to get past that and I think I did." He dropped to his knees before her and grabbed her hands.

"But I am sorry," he said, his voice low and earnest. "It's sorrow, mostly, that I feel. Sorrow for the life *I* could have had, my own lost childhood. And sorrow for you. For the young girl you were when you had to suffer so much."

Marta turned her head away, trying not to see him, not to hear him. Trying not to feel anything.

"But Marta, it's not guilt now." Dominic was ardent. "It's not sorrow now. I don't look at you and feel sorry for the life I took away, the other life you might have had, because I don't see that. No one can see that. You don't let people."

He reached out and touched her hair, and she shook her head and his hand pulled back.

"How can I feel sorry for a life you might have had when you are so alive right now, alive and vital, and beautiful, and strong. When now you are everything I could ever want in someone." He paused. "Marta?"

She couldn't look at him. She couldn't bear it. The two halves of her were tearing her apart. Part of her yearned for him, heard the words he was saying. And the other part boiled. Years of anger and frustration. And pain. Years of asking why. She was like a storm cloud building an electrical charge and he was the lightning rod, and if she just let go, just a little bit, it would all come out and burn him into ashes.

"Marta!" Justin's voice broke across the air.

He was running at them from the direction of the house. Wearing shorts. Out for a jog, Marta thought automatically.

He came up to them panting, paused a moment, and then ran all the way over, his face concerned. And angry.

"Marta," he said, walking up behind her, putting his hand heavily, possessively, on her shoulder. She did not shake it off. And Dominic saw.

"Is everything all right?" It was hardly a question. Justin's voice was edged like a knife.

Dominic looked up and met his eyes. Then he looked at Marta. She did not speak, and finally he looked down. At his hands on her arms. And he dropped his head and his hands from her at the same time. Then he stood and backed away. He nodded.

He looked up at Marta once more, his eyes black as tar, black with sorrow. "If only I had known then what it would cost me now," he said. Then he turned and walked away.

Roan found Billy under the boardwalk. She shook him roughly awake.

"I need a place," she said when he opened his eyes. "It's me, Roan," she smiled. "I need a place," she said again. "A different place. She knows about this one. She's been here before."

Billy sat up and brushed the sand from his hair and wiped his eyes. He reached into his pocket and pulled out a crumpled joint and a book of matches.

"Toke?" His voice was low and choked.

Roan grabbed the matchbook from his hand.

"No!" she said frantically. "Not now! Listen, man, Billy, I really need someplace, I really need someplace now!" She was tugging on his sleeve, glancing over her shoulder every few seconds.

"Okay, okay," Billy said. "I've got a friend."

Billy looked at her again, slowly.

"Yeah." Billy smiled. "He'll help you out. He'll *love* you."

TWENTY

Her head was moving back and forth the way it was supposed to, and Kate had her eye on everyone on the beach in front of her, but her mind was definitely elsewhere. What a morning! She still couldn't get over the scene in the kitchen between Grace and Bo. For the first time in a long time, she didn't have a strong opinion about a situation. But maybe this one was too close to home.

This one isn't close, it's in your home, Quinn, she reminded herself. Maybe Grace wasn't Kate's favorite person in the world. But then again, Bo had never been her soul mate. It was a sticky situation, Kate thought. It's always difficult when one person tries to help another. Especially when the other person doesn't think they need any help.

"Help!" someone screamed.

Kate sat up like a shot. She looked around frantically, trying to locate the problem as she slipped from her chair and jumped to the sand below her.

"Ouch!" she screamed as her legs crumpled below her. She fell, rolling, onto the sand. Suddenly she was surrounded.

"What's wrong?"

"Is she okay?"

"What happened?"

"Did someone push her?"

There were strange hands in her armpits, and she was lifted into a sitting position. Kate looked down at her right foot, covered in blood.

"Help!" she heard the screaming again, and craned her neck until she saw a pretty blond girl laughing and falling from a pair of strong brown shoulders into a forest of strong brown arms.

Kate shook her head and looked back down at her feet.

Someone wiped away the sand and blood and Kate saw a small piece of broken white shell stuck in the ball of her foot. She reached down and yanked it out.

"You'll have to get stitches for that, young lady," an elderly woman said, standing over Kate and shaking a finger in her face.

"Guard down!" she heard the yell of one of

her fellow lifeguards. He was over at her chair, and he turned to signal the guards on either side of her. He came jogging over.

"Hey, Quinn," he said, laughing. "Tough day on patrol? Watch out for those drowning seashells."

"Very funny," she snapped as he put out a hand and pulled her to her feet.

"Go on to the clinic," he said, reaching into his waist pouch and pulling on a pair of mirrored sunglasses. "I'll keep your chair warm for the rest of the afternoon."

"Will I need stitches?" Kate winced as Marta swabbed the cut in her foot with a vibrant orange liquid.

Marta bent over and gently pressed around the cut.

"It's swelling a little," she said, "but I think we got all the sand out."

"What do you think?" Kate asked, her voice low.

Marta laughed. "No stitches, but plenty of aspirin. Sometimes stitches can cause an infection, because they can trap dirt or germs beneath the skin."

Kate wrinkled her nose. "That's gross," she said. "But you enjoy this stuff, don't you, Marta?" she said knowingly. "You enjoy talking about dirty germs trapped under layers of bloody skin. Ugh!"

Marta laughed again. "You're a good patient, Kate. Now let me bandage this up and you'll be set."

Marta wrapped Kate's foot in layers of clean white gauze and made a small bag for her to take home.

"A few dressing changes. To keep it clean."

"I have to clean it myself?" Kate gasped. "Don't I get in-home care? Isn't that one of the perks of living with an almost doctor?"

Ming knocked, and pushed open the door to the examining room.

"Marta," he said, "are you about done? Your lunch date is here. And he doesn't look like the kind of guy who wants to be kept waiting." Ming winked.

Marta turned and wheeled herself out of the examining room. Kate came limping behind her.

"Lunch date?" Marta asked. "I don't have a lunch date—"

She stopped as she rounded the corner to the waiting room. Kate ran into her, and then looked up and saw why Marta had stopped.

"Justin—" Marta and Kate said at the same time.

Marta quickly wheeled forward, her eyes wide, shaking her head imperceptibly, telling him it was all right to make a joke about the lunch date, come up with some other excuse to be there.

But he just smiled as she came closer.

"I thought I might take you to lunch," he said to Marta. Then he looked up.

"Hi, Kate," Justin said calmly. "What happened? Did you hurt yourself?"

"I cut my foot," Kate replied

Marta wasn't speaking. She didn't know quite what to say. Part of her felt like a pawn. She sensed that something was still going on between Kate and Justin and she was getting stuck in the middle of it. *You like Justin,* she told herself. *Yes, and I also like Kate,* she answered. *And I don't particularly like this being how she finds out.*

Finds out what? she asked herself. *That there's something between you and Justin?*

"I'm sorry to hear that," Justin said, his voice genuine. "Are you free now?" he asked, turning back to Marta and putting a hand on her shoulder.

"Sure," Marta replied quickly. "Let me get my bag," and she turned and rolled away down the hall.

Kate watched Marta leave. Then she turned back to Justin and tried to smile.

"You're going to lunch with Marta?" she asked, hoping her voice wasn't betraying her. "That's nice. I really like her."

"Thanks for the approval," Justin said wryly. "I like her too."

Kate blushed, angry and embarrassed at herself.

"Well, I've got to get home," she said quickly. "The doctor told me I needed to rest."

Outside, she almost fell onto her knees. She stumbled over to the railing and leaned on it for a second, and then straightened quickly, afraid that Marta and Justin might follow her out. She turned and started limping home.

"What's wrong with you?" she cried to herself. "What's wrong with you, you gave him up! You didn't want him, so why are you so sad that he's seeing someone else?"

That was a nice way to put it, she thought. She wasn't sad. She was devastated.

"Marta," Justin said, coming up behind her and leaning down over her shoulder. "Marta? Are you okay?"

He'd followed her down the hall into her office, where she was going aimlessly through her bag, her hands trembling.

Justin turned her chair around to face him.

"I know I haven't done this before, but trust me, okay?" he said, sliding his hands below her legs and lifting her into his arms. He carried her to the examining table and set her down.

"I'm sorry about that," Justin said, sighing and running a hand through his hair. "I guess I came at a bad time, huh?"

Marta nodded.

"I guess," she said softly.

"But I would still like to take you to lunch." Justin put a finger under her chin and lifted her face up. "In a minute."

He lowered his head to hers and kissed her.

TWENTY-ONE

Roan looked around the bathroom wildly. *What am I going to do?* she asked herself frantically. This was a big mistake. Billy's friend Rick had pushed her into the bathroom.

"Why don't you freshen up?" he'd said, reaching out and petting her hair. "You can stay here as long as you need to." He'd grinned at her wickedly.

"And then you can come out and meet my friends. You help me," Rick had added crudely, "and you can stay here as long as you want."

His "friends" were two strange men in the living room setting up a video camera. They'd leered at her and nodded to Rick as he'd led her past them.

"She's hot," one of them had said.

"And she looks like she knows how to play,"

the other had answered, his voice a low laugh.

Roan locked the bathroom door.

"Hey, honey," Rick called from the other side. "Are you done yet? We're all anxious to get to know you."

Roan turned both taps on in the sink.

"I'll be right out," she answered shakily.

There was a window, but it looked small. She went over to it and tried to push it up, but it was stuck.

"Calm down," she whispered to herself. "Get a grip."

She tried it again, loosened it, and put her shoulder beneath the sill. She shoved and it gave, squeaking up. She pushed out the screen and got up on the toilet. She saw that at least her head would fit.

Rick knocked again.

"Come on, baby," he said. "Don't keep us waiting too much longer."

Roan tossed her bag out the window. She put her head out, squeezed her shoulders through, and looked down. It was about ten feet to the ground below. She kept squirming, and the banging on the door grew louder. She got her arms free and held herself out against the house. The window ledge scraped her stomach and her hips. But then she felt the release as her legs slid through the window and she fell.

* * *

Kate found her key and went to open the front door, but it was already unlocked. Of course, she thought happily. Tosh would be home. She hadn't been looking forward to being in the empty house after what she'd seen at the clinic.

The clinic. Maybe she just needed to see Tosh and she would feel better.

"Just see him," she said aloud. "And let him hold you. He always says the right thing, anyway."

She went inside and dropped her small beach bag by the front door and kicked off her one sandal. Her foot was starting to hurt again.

She limped up the carpeted stairs quietly. She wondered what Tosh was up to. Probably lying on the bed, reading. He'd be able to get her mind off things. And *he'd* be happy for her company, at least.

If Kate had paused just for a moment before going into her room, she probably never would have opened the door. But she was deep in her own thoughts, and by the time the sounds coming from her bedroom had registered, the door swung aside and Kate saw for herself what Tosh was up to. And that he wasn't reading. And that he wasn't thinking of her. And she didn't imagine he would be able to say the right thing. Or that he would be happy for her company.

Tosh had already found someone to keep him company.

And her name wasn't Kate.

Although she was wearing one of Kate's nightgowns.

And lying with him in Kate's bed.

Roan ran across the lobby, but Rick was after her in an instant. She tripped, and screamed as she felt Rick's hand on her back, and she turned and clawed his face with her fingernails and scrambled away.

She was looking behind her as the bathroom door opened, and she ran into a dark-haired man who was coming out. He grabbed her, and she started screaming. She saw Rick's hand go into his pocket. He flicked his wrist as it came out, and then he was holding a knife.

"You bitch," he yelled, and lunged.

Roan closed her eyes, waiting for the pain. She heard the sound of other people screaming, and someone calling out for the police, but all she felt were the arms that held her pushing hard. And then she was spinning away.

"Thanks for lunch," Marta said as Justin held the door of the clinic for her.

"No problem," Justin replied.

Marta wheeled herself into the waiting room. No one was behind the desk.

"I wonder where everybody is," she said.

She wheeled behind the counter and was about to turn down the hall when Ming came tearing past her, almost knocking her over.

"Thank God you're here," he cried. "Emergency. Come on."

There wasn't time to argue. Ming grabbed her chair and spun her around and pushed her rapidly to the back of the building.

"Ambulance?" Marta asked as they pushed through the doors to the parking lot.

The ambulance screeched to a halt, and two paramedics jumped out and ran to the back. They pulled open the doors and grabbed the gurney inside and slid it out. Marta saw a flash of white sheet, blood seeping through, and dark black hair. Then Roan stumbled out of the back, and Marta gasped. Roan was covered in blood, and she was wailing.

"Roan!" Marta screamed.

"She's fine!" Ming yelled at her. "He's the one we have to save," he said, pushing her behind the gurney. They slid into the operating room behind the paramedics. The white sheet was turning deep red.

"Knife wound to the stomach," one of the paramedics said.

"Set up an I.V.," the other barked.

Marta rolled quickly past the body, and turned to look. Then her mouth dropped, and she almost ran into the wall. That wasn't a stranger lying on the operating table.

It was Dominic.